LINDY: A FANTASY

JEREMY LUKE HILL

Vocamus Press
Guelph, Ontario

Written by Jeremy Luke Hill
Some rights reserved

Cover Art by Larisa Koshkina
Public Domain

ISBN 13: 978-0-9880176-1-0 (hbk)
ISBN 13: 978-0-9880176-0-3 (pbk)
ISBN 13: 978-0-9880176-2-7 (pdf)

VP

Vocamus Press
130 Dublin Street, North
Guelph, Ontario, Canada
N1H 4N4

www.vocamus.net

2012

For my children.

— 1 —

In Which Some Introductions are Made

Once there was a town that had been small for a very long time but was getting bigger and had just become that comfortable size that is the greatest time in the history of any town. It had some little shops, and a skating rink, and a town hall, and some lovely old churches, and several schools for children of different ages, and a small university for the oldest children. It did not have a loud highway running through it, or big factories, or super-stores, but it did very well without these things, and no one felt the need for them.

Near the edge of this town, there was a street called Devonshire. It followed a stretch of railway track that made its way from the main line toward the town's old train station. Devonshire was mostly an ordinary street except that it had been built on both sides of the track rather than just on one side or the other. This meant that the trains ran down the middle, and the cars drove on either side, so the children sometimes had to wait a long time before the street was clear enough to visit their friends across the way.

Though the street was a little different, most of the houses on Devonshire were of a regular sort. They were small, square, and brick, and they had become a bit shabby over the years. Their windows and doors needed paint, and their roofs looked leaky in places, and their fences leaned one way or the other as they chose. Because they were small and in bad repair, they were also cheap, and so the people who lived in them tended to be of two sorts: those who were down on their luck but were working very hard to make the best of it, and those who were down on their luck and were giving up hope that things would ever get better. The houses of the first sort seemed a little neater, even if the roofs still leaked, but the houses of the second sort had trash on the lawn, or smashed porch lights, or broken bicycles in the driveway that no one bothered to fix.

There was one house on the street, however, that was not at all small and not at all shabby, even though it was very old. It had been the farmhouse when the whole street and everything around it had been farmland, and it had gradually been closed in, first by the railway that was laid along the road, then by the station that was built for the nearby town, and then, all of a sudden, by all the houses that were built as the town became a city.

The farmhouse was built all of grey stone, and there had been additions made to it several times, so that it had an irregular sort of shape, some parts having two stories, and others parts having three, and the part at the back having only one. Its windows were also of different shapes and sizes, and the roof was at different angles depending on the place. The whole house seemed as if it had been thrown together over the years without any thought as to how it might look, which was very likely the case.

Not only was the farmhouse the biggest house on the street, but it also had the biggest lot, which was big enough for five or six houses. Everything was surrounded by a stone wall that kept all but the tallest of people from seeing over it, so the house always seemed a bit mysterious, especially to the children of the street, who made up all sorts of stories about it.

What made these stories seem true was the man who lived in the house, who looked strange enough for any story the children might think to tell. He was a few years older than middle age, and he had long, grey hair, which was normal enough, but he wore shabby, old-fashioned clothes that looked like they came from someone's attic, and no matter what the season, no matter what the weather, he always had on a black, three-cornered hat, like the pirates in stories wear, all battered and worn around the edges. Because he always wore this hat, the children called him Mister Hat, even though they knew that his name was really Mister Owen. They did not

3

know whether to be afraid of him or not. They had all been told by their parents that they were not to speak to strangers, which is a very good rule, and Mister Hat was quite strange indeed, and he lived in a mysterious house besides, but he also smiled at everyone when he met them on the street, and he would touch his hat with a little bow to them, even to the smallest of the children.

If they had asked their parents about him, the children might have learned that Mister Hat was even stranger than they thought. Even the adults who had lived on the street the longest, and some had lived there for many years, could not remember a time when Mister Owen had not lived in the old farmhouse. It seemed as though he had always lived there, and it seemed as though he had always been old, or, at least, that he had always been as old as he was, which, as I said, was just past middle age.

When the adults bothered to think about Mister Owen at all, they would always say how odd it was that he never seemed to get any older, but nobody really gave it too much thought. Mister Owen kept mostly to himself, and the adults mostly forgot that they even had such an odd neighbour. The children, however, never forgot how odd their neighbour really was. They loved his peculiar clothes, his slow and royal walks, and the way that he would touch his hat to them as if they were not children at all. When he walked through the neighbourhood, they would run ahead of him and wait in line for the bow he always gave them, so that it looked as if Mister Owen was a general reviewing some motley regiment of toy soldiers, or perhaps a giant of a king making a parade among his tiny subjects. He seemed to enjoy their attention, saying a grave "Good day" to them now and again, and most often taking his walk in the afternoon, just after school was finished for the day, so that he could be sure of meeting the children as they came home.

One girl in particular, whose name was Lindy, loved to watch for Mister Hat. She lived just to the right of his house, close enough that she could hear the creaking of the big iron gates at the end of his driveway whenever he opened them. Whether she was playing in her backyard or doing schoolwork or helping around the house, Lindy always listened for the creak of those gates. When she heard them, she would race to the end of her driveway so that Mister Hat could give his bow and perhaps wish her a good day. Even though he dressed strangely, there was something about Mister Hat that made Lindy feel happier whenever she saw him, and she was quite sure that he was not as crazy as people said he was. When he passed her on the street and they exchanged their greeting, she would be cheerful for the rest of the day, doing her chores without complaining and singing to herself as she did her schoolwork, but if she heard that she had missed one of Mister Hat's walks, she would be disappointed and might forget her chores or her homework altogether, and her mother would sometimes ask what had gotten into her.

Some days, if Mister Hat took his walk early enough in the afternoon, and if there was a long while until supper, Lindy would follow him a ways, making sure to stay out of sight. She would often follow right to the end of the block, across the one-way street, and through the little park with the band stand and the fountain, until Mister Hat crossed the main road, where Lindy's mother did not allow her to go. It was not that Mister Hat did anything so very interesting that made Lindy follow him. He would just walk along with his slow, firm steps, very tall and grand, sometimes twirling his silver-headed walking stick, and sometimes smoking on the pipe that he kept in his jacket pocket. He never stopped to do anything at all and never said anything more than "Good day." Still, Lindy felt that there was something mysterious about him, as if he might suddenly turn into a bird and fly away or disappear into thin air, if only she watched him long enough. Of course, he never did either of these things, but Lindy liked to think that he might all the same.

Now, just because Lindy imagined these sorts of things, I would not want you thinking her the kind of girl who spent all her time daydreaming, for she was quite the opposite. She was on the whole a very responsible girl, especially considering that she was only twelve years old at the time of our story. She was usually very good about doing her homework and helping around the house, and she had even begun babysitting for some of her neighbours, who would tell Lindy's mother how lucky she was to have such a dependable daughter.

Indeed, Lindy's mother, whose name was Missus Merton, often had to remind Lindy that she did not need to be quite so serious all the time. She would see Lindy reading in the livingroom or practising on the old piano, and she would tell her to go and play with her friends. So, Lindy would go, just to make her mother happy, even though she would much rather have played by herself.

Her favourite thing to do was to climb the steep stairway to the attic, through the boxes of summer clothes and Christmas decorations, to her cubby, the dormer window that faced the house where Mister Hat lived. It was probably not the sort of place that you or I would choose to spend our time. It smelled musty, especially in warmer weather, and the light was dim, even with a reading lamp, and it had more than a few spiders. It was also cold in the winter, so that Lindy had to wear a sweater and wrap herself in blankets just to stay warm, but despite all of these things, she loved the dormer. She loved it because it was quiet and because it was dark, but most of all because she could just be by herself.

She also loved it because she could look out across Mister Hat's garden, which was quite beautiful, especially in the spring and fall, even though Mister Hat did not keep it very tidy. It had almost a forest of trees along the stone wall, more trees around the house, and an apple orchard at the back. It also had some broad, open spaces that looked like they had once been better tended,

7

with flagstone walkways and benches and statues and a big stone arch that had ivy growing up it. Everything was overgrown with bushes and plants, but it was still beautiful in a wild sort of way, and Lindy liked the view from her dormer window very much.

In the summer, however, the attic would eventually become so hot that Lindy had to go out to the backyard elm tree when she wanted time alone. The elm grew very close to Mister Hat's wall, so she could climb to the top of the wall and sit on it, dangling her feet over the side as she watched the squirrels and the rabbits in the garden. Because of the trees in Mister Hat's yard, she was well hidden from view, and she spent much of her summer holidays reading in this very spot, which perhaps accounts for the fact that she just happened to be there one day when a most peculiar thing happened.

— 2 —

In Which There is an Odd Incident Involving Mister Hat

It was one of those days very early in the summer when it is warm enough for shorts in the sun but cool enough for a jacket in the shade. There were already leaves on the trees that grew along Mister Hat's wall, but they were still a light sort of green and still delicate enough that Lindy could see sunlight through them as she looked into Mister Hat's garden.

She had begun the day reading in her cubby as usual, and though the weather was not yet so warm that she would have chosen to come down on her own, her mother had come up to chase her into the yard before too long. She was the kind of mother who believes in things like getting fresh air and eating healthy food and going to bed at a decent time and doing enough exercise, and she thought it a shame for Lindy to spend yet another beautiful spring day indoors.

Her Mother had come into the attic, tidying as she went, just as she always did. She was continually tidying, not because she was one of those mothers who cannot have a single thing out of place, but because there was always something to be tidied, and because she was out at work most of the day, so she seldom had the time to do a really proper clean. Besides, she always said that tidying was one of the things that makes a house a home, like cooking and keeping the garden and washing clothes, because money can buy a house, but only work can make it a home.

Lindy's mother, as you might have guessed, was a practical woman. She did not have time for putting herself together, and she did not have money for fancy clothes, so few people would have called her pretty, but she was beautiful in a more sensible and motherly way that had to do with how her mouth was always smiling and how her eyes were always caring and how she never complained about anything. Though she had to work long hours cleaning houses, and though she had been left to look after Lindy all alone, she always went cheerfully about her work, and Lindy knew that it was out of love for her. This is why, when her mother said what a lovely day it was and how she wished that Lindy would spend at least part of it out of doors, Lindy did not complain. She only gave her mother a kiss on the cheek and headed out to sit on the wall in the backyard, where she sat looking out across Mister Hat's yard.

Right beneath her there was a wild looking patch of garden, filled mostly with overgrown rose bushes and different kinds of ivy and some tall plants that had yellow leaves that looked like flowers and other sorts of bushes all grown together in a tangle. Just beyond the bushes there was a path of stones that were nearly covered in moss, and there was also a stone bench that needed very badly to be cleaned before anyone could sit on it. On the other side of the path the plants were shorter, almost like grass, and there were little flowers, blue and yellow and white, shooting through the leaves here and there.

All this Lindy could see very easily, but the rest of the garden was mostly hidden by the branches around her, and she could only see further when a particularly strong breeze blew the leaves far enough aside. When the breeze did blow strongly, which happened every few minutes or so, she could also see the ivy-covered archway standing in the middle of the grass and flowers, looking like an old church doorway but without the church. The stone of the arch was white and pink, like the colour on the inside of some seashells, and it was taller even than the wall, tall enough for two people to go through, one standing on top of the other.

Behind the arch there was another row of trees, but it was the arch that Lindy liked to see best, or rather, she liked to see the trees too, but mostly because she could see them through the arch. She liked to think that the archway was a kind of picture frame, only its picture was real and moving and alive, full of waving trees and falling sunlight and sometimes animals. She looked each time the wind blew to see how the picture through the arch had changed from her last look and from the look before it.

On this particular Saturday, Lindy had been sitting on the wall for most of the morning, leaning against the trunk of the tree, sometimes reading a book, when she heard the breeze begin to rustle the leaves once again. She looked out to see what picture the archway would make, but instead of the trees and flowers that she expected, she saw in the archway what looked like a silvery window or a cloudy mirror, and through the window, she saw the face of a man.

Actually, she could see the whole of the man from head to foot, but it was only his face that she could see clearly, since all the rest of his body was dark somehow, while his face was bright like sunlight. She could not have told you exactly what his face looked like, though she could remember it to herself ever after. She could only say that its colour was like the green of new leaves mixed with the gold of the sun, and that it looked stern in the way that kings are stern in old pictures, not angry, but strong and proud. Indeed, Lindy thought that he might be a king, for there was a sort of crown on his head made from ivy and white flowers that made him look very solemn and kingly and made Lindy feel a little frightened. Then the breeze stopped, and the leaves blocked her view of the archway once more.

Now, I hope you can forgive Lindy for being somewhat frightened at seeing this man standing suddenly in the archway. After all, it is only natural to be frightened by things that are out of the ordinary, and you must admit that it is not at all ordinary for kings to appear without warning in peoples' gardens, shining and green-gold and wearing crowns of flowers. Neither is it ordinary for doors, even tall stone arches that lead nowhere in particular, to turn into windows or mirrors or anything else for that matter. Truthfully, I would have been a bit frightened myself, and you probably would have been too if you had been in her place.

To Lindy's credit, though, she was really only frightened for a minute before she started to feel better again. This was not because she was very brave, though she was certainly one of the braver people I have known. It was because she was very smart, and she quickly came to the reasonable conclusion that her eyes were playing tricks on her and that there really was no silvery window or stern looking king, just the light making the trees look strange or something equally ordinary. So, instead of climbing down the tree and going back to her house, which would have ended our story before it really had a chance to begin, she sat up and began crawling along the wall to a place where she could get a better view.

Of course, when she could see the arch again, it was just as she suspected. It looked normal once more, and the picture it held was only the trees behind it waving gently in the breeze, and there also was Mister Hat, pushing a wheelbarrow of dirt toward the path. The mystery, she thought, was explained. There had been no golden king coming through a mirror, only Mister Hat coming through the arch with his wheelbarrow. She must have imagined all the rest.

Mister Hat did not look up to where Lindy was sitting, and she stayed there for a moment, feeling some relief, but also a little disappointment. However frightening it may have been to see a king suddenly appear in Mister Hat's garden, it was also disappointing to discover that she had been right all along, that there really was no silvery mirror or golden king, and that this morning was as plain and ordinary as any other had been or was likely to be.

As Lindy was thinking these things, Mister Hat emptied the dirt from his wheelbarrow along the far side of the path and turned back toward the arch and the house beyond it, as if he was finished his work for the morning and was going home for his lunch. Then, just as Lindy was thinking that she should probably be heading inside too, Mister Hat did something that made the morning very much less plain and ordinary once more. As he stepped through the arch, it turned silvery again, and there was a moment when his head seemed to be golden and crowned with vines. Then he simply disappeared.

Maybe it was the surprise of seeing someone she knew disappear in the middle of his own garden, or maybe it was the shock of having been proven wrong in all her very reasonable conclusions, but Lindy could not afterwards say exactly why she did what she did. She did not go home, which would surely have been the safer thing to do. Instead, she jumped down into Mister Hat's garden, right in the middle of the overgrown ivies and rosebushes that grew along the wall. She did not think about being frightened, and she certainly did not think about getting her clothes dirty, because the drop was a big one, and she landed in bushes and thorns and dirt, so that she was soon scratched and muddy all over. In fact, she could never remember thinking anything at all, which is probably why she could do something as brave and silly as jump from such a height into a thicket of thorns and brambles in someone else's garden.

From where she had landed, there were still several yards of bushes between her and the stone path, so she had gathered a good many more scratches and even some tears in her clothes by the time she was free of them and stood beside the stone bench, seeing the archway from a much nearer distance than she had ever seen it before. Now that she was this close, however, she did have some time to think, and she began to realize how silly a thing it was for her to go any further, especially if someone really had just disappeared not far away. On the other hand, she was curious, and she could not bring herself to go home just yet either, so there she stood, afraid to go further but unwilling to go back.

If you had asked Lindy just then what exactly she was planning to do, she might have said something like, "I guess I'm waiting for Mister Hat to come back." Of course, you were not there to ask her any such thing, so she just kept standing by the bench, looking into the archway where Mister Hat had disappeared. She waited for what seemed to her a very long time, but Mister Hat did not return, and she began to think that perhaps she had imagined everything after all, though she did not really believe this.

How long she might have waited there, and what she might have decided to do in the end are both things we will never know, however, because just then, Lindy heard the sound of feet in the garden a little way off, and she saw three figures coming toward her, two men and a woman. They were all dressed strangely, like characters from a movie about knights and ladies, and Lindy felt immediately that there was something wrong about them. They were looking around as if searching for something, or as if worried that something was searching for them, and they were making straight for where Lindy was standing.

She felt a tingling kind of fear, like she had never felt before, and without realizing exactly what she was doing, she backed away from them toward the archway until she bumped into one of its pink pillars. As soon as she touched the stone, there was a kind of humming, low and soft, and she turned to see that the arch was filled again with silver and grey.

When Lindy had watched Mister Hat from the wall, the archway had looked like a cloudy mirror or a silvered window, but now that she was closer, it looked more like thick smoke, blue and grey, swirling about between two panes of glass, and in the smoke there were flecks of gold like tiny stars, shining out for a moment, then hidden in the smoke, then shining once again. She felt all of a sudden as though she had always known about the arch, with its silvery smoke and swirling lights, as if she had always known that she would pass through it some day. It seemed to her that she was remembering all these things from long ago, and just when she thought this, she was drawn through the smoke and into something else altogether.

— 3 —

In Which Lindy Meets Some People She Does Not Expect

Afterwards, Lindy was never sure if she actually stepped through the archway at all. In her memory it always seemed that the archway came and passed over her, or that the panes of glass disappeared and let the smoke envelope her. The gold flecks grew and shone more brightly, and a whole sky of stars spun around her, all trailing great wisps and ribbons of silver mist. She could still see bits of the trees and the grass here and there, but they were just patches of green whirling through the gold and the blue and the grey.

After a time that seemed both very long and very short, the spots of green became larger, and the stars became smaller and more distant, and the swirling smoke became more still. Then, all at once, the mist passed away from her, and she stood once more beneath the arch, its shell-pink stone stretching over her, and the trees swaying around her.

For a moment she thought that perhaps nothing had changed at all. The trees were all in their places, and Mister Hat's house was still where it had been just a few moments earlier, but she soon realized that some other things had changed very much indeed. She was no longer standing in the overgrown grass of the garden. Instead, she and the arch were both in the centre of a broad circle of stone. It looked a little like the low stage of the bandstand in the park, but it was the same colour as the arch, and it was more suited for a palace than for a park or a garden.

There were also, she now noticed, a cluster of stone cottages that had sprung up in the orchard behind Mister Hat's house. They were nestled closely together, filling the whole back of the yard, and they mingled with the fruit trees as naturally as the grass and the flowers. Cobblestone pathways joined the gates of their low garden walls, weaving between the trees and climbing the small hills with flights of stairs. Everything was so intermingled that it was difficult to tell where one yard ended and another began. It was as if the houses had seeded and sprouted there, growing slowly out of the landscape over the years.

Lindy felt drawn to the cottages as soon as she saw them. She walked across the stone platform and along the cobble path that ran toward the little houses, until she was looking over the walls into their gardens and peering as closely through the windows as she dared. She found an old well in the open place in the middle of the cottages, and a big stone oven beside the path that ran away from them toward the house, and a long low barn on the further side of them. All the while, she felt more and more that the cottages had just grown there with the trees, and that she was somehow a part of the growing.

It was all very beautiful to Lindy, but there was a kind of sadness about the garden too, a kind of emptiness. The cottages were tended. The roofs were in good repair, and the paint on the doors and the shutters looked fresh, but there were no faces in the windows, no gardeners in the gardens, and no walkers on the pathways. Everything was still. Even Mister Hat's house seemed emptier than it had before. The whole garden seemed to be remembering when there had been people living in it and to be waiting for others to come and live in it again. The feeling of sadness was in the stillness and the remembering and the waiting.

As she grew used to her surroundings, Lindy also began to notice something that was more difficult for her to describe. "Everything," she told me later, "was somehow more perfect, even though it looked exactly the same as it did before."

"So, for example," I suggested, "the trees were taller and straighter?"

"No, no," she said, "That's not it at all. The short things and the crooked things were still short and crooked. They were just properly short and crooked. They were properly tall and short and leafy and bare and straight and crooked and, well, they were properly trees, you know?"

I was not sure that I did know, but maybe you will, so I will try as much as I can to describe things exactly as she did. According to Lindy, most of the garden looked much like it had before. It was as wild and as overgrown as it had ever been, but everything now seemed exactly where it was meant to be. It was as if Lindy could now see what Mister Hat's garden had really been all the time, as if she could now understand the reason why each tree and flower was growing where it was.

She had been wandering for some time, surrounded by this strange and beautiful new garden, when she was startled by the sound of a door opening at the side of Mister Hat's house. Her first thought was that something else extraordinary was about to happen, and she turned toward the house almost certain that she would find a giant or a centaur or something equally fantastic walking across the lawn. The two men who came through the door, however, were not particularly extraordinary. True, one was a little taller and thinner than the average person, but he was certainly no giant, and the other was the most regular sort of man there could be.

Even so, Lindy was a little frightened. She had been

expecting to meet only Mister Hat when she had jumped into the garden, and everything had felt so empty after she had gone through the arch that she had not expected to meet anyone at all. Now there were two strangers approaching her, and she began to wonder whether they would accuse her of trespassing or take her back to her mother or something even worse.

With all this going through her mind, I think you will understand why she considered trying to run, and she did consider it very seriously for a moment, but she knew that the wall was too high for her to climb and that the men would probably catch her before she could even try, so she decided to be as cooperative as she could and hope that they would let her go with just a warning.

As they drew nearer, she could see them more clearly, and she began to think that perhaps they were not so ordinary after all. The taller man was really quite tall, and he was dressed in heavy leather clothes that looked handmade by someone who had no idea whatsoever how to sew. They made him look like a castaway from a desert island, and he would have been quite frightening indeed if he had not been smiling in so a friendly way and if he had not given Lindy a little wave as he grew closer.

The smaller man was also not as regular as she had first thought him to be. He was very bald, and he wore a fancy suit with long tails at the back and white gloves and shiny black shoes, like a magician without the top hat. He was walking very carefully through the grass, keeping his shoes and pants clean, hardly even looking in Lindy's direction, but when he did look up, he did not smile at all, though he did not exactly frown either. He looked like maybe he had forgotten how to smile or frown altogether, and he did not at all seem the sort of man who let people off with warnings, but it was too late to run, so she just waited and hoped.

When the two men approached her, the shorter man in the fancy clothes bowed very deeply, cleared his throat, and said, "Miss Lindy, if I may presume to address you before the proper introductions have been made, Mister Alisdair Bridgebane has instructed me..."

"Actually," the taller man interrupted, still smiling, "Alisdair only asked, really. He isn't the sort of person who orders people around much." He looked even taller now that he was close, and he was looming over the shorter man's shoulder from a rather alarming height.

The shorter man stopped in the middle of his sentence and looked up at his companion for a moment before turning back to Lindy. "I hope," he continued, "that Miss Lindy will forgive Osborne's appalling manners. Despite my very best efforts during my tenure as butler in Mister Bridgebane's service, the staff are still undisciplined, inappropriate, and even, in some cases," he paused for emphasis, "insubordinate."

Osborne chuckled in a low and friendly way. "Don't worry," he said, "Eddie always talks like that. Big words make him happy."

23

The shorter man ignored him. "As I was saying, Mister Alisdair Bridgebane has instructed me," he paused and looked back at Osborne once more, "to inform you that he is saddened to be unable to receive you personally, though it would have been his very great pleasure. Unfortunately, matters of some importance have required his immediate attention. He has instructed," and the shorter man emphasized this word just slightly more than was necessary, "that I am to make every effort to arrange for your comfortable stay here at The Crofts." He bowed again. "Have you any personal effects with which Osborne might assist you?"

He gestured to Osborne at the end of this speech, and the larger man bent forward in an overly elaborate bow, his hand fluttering as low as he could reach, near his knee somewhere. "At your service Miss," he said in his pleasant way, "especially since you don't seem to need it." He stood upright again. "That's the easiest sort of service to offer, you know, the kind that won't be accepted anyway."

The smaller man managed to look annoyed without actually changing his expression.

"Osborne is really my family name," the tall man continued. "My first name is Morris. Everyone calls me Moe, except old Eddie here."

"My name," the smaller man said, in a tone that managed to be both emotionless and offended all at once, "is Clinton Edward Beale. If you have need of my services,

24

you should address me as Clinton."

"I would have let him introduce himself," Moe said, "only he thinks it's rude."

"It is rude, in fact," said Clinton, sounding as if he was explaining something for the hundredth time, "especially in the case of one's social superiors."

Moe seemed not to hear him. Instead, he offered Lindy his large and surprisingly gentle hand. Lindy shook it, then offered her own to Clinton in turn. He hesitated for a moment and then shook it, once, briskly.

Lindy had not yet had a chance to say anything during all of this, and she felt a bit confused by everything that was happening to her. It seemed that Moe and Clinton were not taking her back to her mother after all, and they were treating her nicely enough, but she had no idea who this Mister Bridgebane was or why he would send people to greet her. Still, she did manage to say, "Good to meet you both," without any difficulty, so she felt that she had not behaved too badly. Unfortunately, both Moe and Clinton seemed to be expecting something more from her.

"You will need," said Clinton at last, "to accept formally the hospitality of the house. However things are done where you come from, around here the formalities must be observed."

"Oh," said Lindy. "What exactly do I say to, um, accept your hospitality, or whatever you said?"

Clinton looked as if he was trying very hard to be

patient. "You need only say something to the effect that you do indeed accept the hospitality of our house."

"Oh," said Lindy again, though she did not normally talk in this silly way. "I do then. Accept your hospitality, I mean."

"Very good," said Clinton. "Follow me if you please," and he began leading the way toward the house of Mister Hat.

4

In Which There Are Still More Surprises

Lindy remembered almost nothing about the walk to the house. She did remember coming through the side door into a room that was just big enough to have a coat closet and a wooden shoe rack and an old hot water radiator. It was dim, but the door to the next room was ajar, and there was a light escaping warmly from around it, and with the light there came the sound of a ladle stirring and the smell of bread baking. It was all very familiar somehow. It was as though she had walked with Clinton and Morris through that room a thousand times but was only just now remembering it, and she knew at once that whatever lay behind the door was something good and safe. The house itself seemed to tell her so.

This is why she was not surprised when Clinton wiped his feet very carefully on the mat, or when he opened the door without really touching it, or even when he began to look very unlike the Clinton that she had just met. She already knew somehow that the light from the open door would seem to burn away his very clean clothes and his very white skin and his very bald head. She already knew that the light would leave him full with a kind of glowing, as if every colour had come together to make him into something that was brighter than white and darker than black. The house whispered all these things to her, and it whispered also that there was no need for her to be afraid.

Clinton turned back to Lindy and motioned for her to follow him. His face still looked much as she remembered it, but it was different now too. It reminded her of pictures of her grandfather as a boy, where the face of the boy in the picture and the face of her grandfather looked the same and different at the same time. The new Clinton and the old one were just like that. They were the same person, but their faces were from different times and places.

Lindy started to follow the new Clinton through the door, but she suddenly remembered that Morris was behind her. Though she knew what she would find even as she turned, the sight of the new Moe was still frightening. His leather clothes had become a heavy and sagging skin that draped over his lean body, while his hands and his feet and his head had grown even larger than they had been before, as if they were meant for a taller and broader body. His face was wider too, like a frog's, but it had a few strands of hair and a mouth filled with teeth that made him look much more fearsome than any frog. Even though Lindy knew that he was the same Morris who had been so friendly to her, she still felt a little scared.

Moe slowly reached out his huge hand, with its long nails and webbed fingers, and patted her shoulder. His new mouth widened into a smile. "It's alright, Miss Lindy," he said, "I wouldn't blame you for having a good scream, ugly thing like me following behind you. Should've warned you, of course. Only we're all so used to each other that we forget."

"It's okay," said Lindy, though she was not quite sure that this was true. "I know you wouldn't hurt me. The house told me so."

"Well," said Moe, "the house has never talked to me, but it's true there's nothing to be scared of, not here in the house. Plenty that'll make you shake your head the first time you see it, of course, but nothing that'll do you harm. Just don't trust the look of things. That's my advice. Nothing is ever what it seems to be here, not for long anyway."

Lindy nodded, and Moe smiled his smile. He shuffled toward the doorway where Clinton was still waiting, and Lindy followed them through the door and down a few steps into a room that she already knew would be the kitchen. It was bigger than any kitchen that she had ever seen, probably bigger than her whole house, and it was set low into the ground so that its doors were halfway up the walls with little stairways leading to them, and its windows were all very high, like windows sometimes are in old churches. There was a huge fireplace with a fire burning, and there were big stone ovens where the bread was baking, and there were wood stoves with pots boiling on them too, so the kitchen felt very warm indeed, but it was the comforting kind of warmth that kitchens have after a cold walk, and Lindy felt right away that she was welcome and at home. There were cupboards and counters everywhere, and there were pots hanging from ceiling racks, and there were sacks and barrels piled wherever there was space, and in the middle of everything there was a huge wooden table surrounded by mismatched chairs and benches.

The house was whispering even more clearly now, though its whispers were more like pictures than words. The pictures were of the kitchen, with its copper pans and its hanging vegetables and its steaming pots, but it was full of people too, so many people that they were often in the same places at the same times, as if she was seeing all the people who had ever been in the kitchen all together at the same moment. They were eating at the table and cooking at the stoves and working at the counters, and they all blended together, and they came and went, and their faces changed from one to another, but the kitchen stayed the same, and Lindy knew that she was in the heart of the house, where it was strongest and warmest and deepest.

Now, I have not really been describing the kitchen in the same way as Lindy saw it, because I have so far left out the one thing that she could not help but see first, even as the house was whispering to her so strongly. In the midst of that warm and fragrant kitchen, taking bread from the stone oven with a long wooden peel, was a most singular cook. Stripped to the waist except for an apron, with thick hair curling over his back and arms, he was both very wide and very short, and Lindy would have called him a dwarf, except the house told her that he was not.

"Hello Penates," said Moe. "Here's our visitor. Her name is Lindy."

"Hello Lindy," said the cook, though he did not stop even long enough to glance at her. He kept moving from one thing to the next, dusting the fresh bread with flour, stirring something in the big pot on the hearth, cutting vegetables on the long wooden counter, and he talked as quickly as he worked. "Are you hungry? Supper's not for a bit. Soup's ready, though. May as well try the bread too. Never taste better than it will right now."

Now that Penates had mentioned it, Lindy did feel a bit hungry, so she said that she would love some soup and bread if that was okay, and Penates said that it would be no trouble at all. He did not seem to interrupt the flow of his work, but he quickly brought a bowl of soup and a heel of bread that were far too large for her eat by herself, and Lindy was soon relishing the tastes of thick, homemade butter and warm, brown bread and dark, onion broth.

"Has Alisdair returned?" asked Clinton. "It would be best if he were to take charge of our visitor himself."

"No," replied Penates, dicing some carrots very small. "I can't feel him in the house. But these things can take some time, depending on what the problem is." He turned to stir something simmering on the stove. "Moe," he called, "get another goose from the cellar, will you? Can't underfeed the company."

Morris grinned and looked at Lindy. "Only come to the kitchen if you want work," he told her. "Penates won't let you sit around for long."

"If you're not eating, you should be cooking," said Penates as he diced, and he looked up long enough to wink at Lindy, who was working her way through the soup much faster than she had expected.

"Yes, well," said Clinton, "in any case, I will go prepare your room, Miss Lindy. Morris can escort you there when you are finished your meal. And I do apologize for bringing you in through the kitchen entrance. Things are not quite as usual around the house, and we thought it best to bring you in by the shortest way. We certainly intended no offence."

Lindy was not actually sure why she should be offended, but she assured Clinton that she accepted his apology, and he had already left the kitchen before she realized what he meant about preparing her room. She was about to tell Moe that she did not really need to stay the night, but just then the sunlight from the high windows was shadowed, and Lindy looked up to see a flock of birds flying into the kitchen. They looked like little brown songbirds, wrens or sparrows, but Lindy knew as soon as she saw them that there were people in the heart of them. She could already see how they would become taller and more human as they landed, with feathers for hair and with the delicate movements of birds but with human faces and voices.

Even before they had landed, however, Lindy felt that things were not as they should be. Their flight was frantic, and their agitation became still clearer when they fluttered to the ground in a cluster around the table. They all milled together, bobbing their heads like pigeons around the town fountain, their eyes wide and wary.

"Penates!" cried one of them, as she rushed toward the cook. "Shut the house as soon as may be. Danger comes!"

"Cleanna?" the cook asked, dropping his knife in alarm. "Has Alisdair sent you?"

"Yes!" the bird woman replied, still urgent. "He comes as quickly as he can, but the danger comes before. Don't waste a moment."

Penates turned, and he looked much less like a cook now and much more like a hero from one of Lindy's storybooks, sterner and firmer. "Moe," he said, "take Miss Lindy to her room right away. And send Clinton to me if you see him. Quickly now." His voice was very calm, but for the first time since she had entered the house, Lindy was afraid. She did not know what there was to fear exactly, but it was enough for her that Penates and Morris and the house itself seemed suddenly alarmed. Everything was watchful now and careful, and Lindy was frightened to think that something had been able to disquiet the house so quickly. Then she found herself being picked up in Moe's massive hands and rushed along corridors and through doorways, up staircases and across landings, but she could not see any of these things clearly. The house whispered nothing to her now, but she could sense its concern, and her own fear deepened.

At last they arrived in a small room, somewhere deep in the house, and Moe laid her on the bed. He turned to go, assuring her that he would return as soon as he could. A sudden terror went through Lindy at the thought of being left alone in the strange vastness of the house, and she started to cry out for Moe to stay with her, but she found that she could not remember what it was that she wanted to say. Her eyes closed, quite against her will, and she slept.

— 5 —

In Which Lindy Finds a Very Long Stairway

When Lindy woke, the house was calm once more, though it still felt watchful, like the rabbits in the park when they are keeping an eye out. Light was coming through a window above her, but it was too high for her to see through, and it was hard to tell if the light was from a late afternoon or an early morning sun. She wondered if she had slept straight through the night, though her stomach told her it had not been that long.

Her room was quite small, with only a single bed and a dresser for furniture, both carved with leaves. There was also a mirror above the dresser and a painting of a tree above the bed, but once she had looked in the mirror to make sure that she was presentable and had looked at the painting for a while, there was nothing much for

35

her to do, and she began to feel a bit bored. Now, she was not one of those children who must be entertained all the time and who cannot live a moment that is not filled by amusements, but she was all alone in that little room, so she can hardly be blamed if she began to wonder whether it might be alright for her to have a look around the house. She could not remember anyone telling her otherwise, and the house seemed not to object when she tried to ask it, so she opened her door and peeked out into the hallway. Everything was deserted, and she was beginning to feel hungry again, so she decided to see if she could find the kitchen and ask Penates whether there was anything for her to eat.

She set off in what she thought was the right direction, but she had to turn one way or another at the end of the hallway, and then to turn again almost immediately afterwards, and then again at the next room, and she was soon very lost indeed. There seemed to be more hallways and stairways than rooms, and the hallways were all somewhat narrow, and there were not really enough lights, so everything seemed a bit cramped and a bit dark and bit mysterious, and Lindy found herself wondering whether she would ever find the kitchen at all.

She was just considering calling for help, when she came into a very wide hallway that was lined with six doors on each side. The doors all had plaques above them with writing in strange black letters that Lindy could not read. The nearest of the doors was half-open, so she could see that it held a little fieldstone fireplace, and a big oak desk, and a leather chair that was quite worn around its brass nailheads. The whole rest of the room was filled with books. It was not a large room, but its walls were entirely covered with shelves, and there were other shelves standing in the middle of it, and Lindy was quite sure that she had never seen so many books in one place before, not even at the public library. She walked into the room and went slowly down the shelves, running her fingers along the spines.

Some of them were very old, with their leather bindings all cracked and broken, but others were almost new, with crisp cloth or paper bindings. Many of the titles were in other languages, and most of the English titles were complicated things like, *On the Perpetuation of Varieties and Species by Natural Means of Selection*, or *An Inquiry into the Nature and Causes of the Wealth of Nations*, or *The History of the Decline and Fall of the Roman Empire*, but there were a few books that Lindy could understand. There was one about Charlemagne, who was a knight in some of the stories that she had read, and there was one about birds, which were her favourite animals, and there was one by Shakespeare, who was the writer of a play that she had read in school. The books did not seem to be in any order that she could see. They were not listed by their authors, or by their titles, or even by their subjects, but she still made sure to put them back exactly where she found them, just in case.

When she went out, she left the door partly open, just as it had been when she had gone in, and she was about to go on to the next door, when she had the curious feeling that she was not alone. It was not a frightening sort of feeling, just the sense that there was someone nearby, and it even made her feel safer in a way, like how she felt better in the dark just knowing that her mother was sleeping only a few steps down the hallway.

"Hello?" she called, but there was no answer, only the sound of pages turning behind her. She turned back into the room and saw that a book now lay open on the desk with words appearing on its pages as if written by an invisible hand. She edged back into the room toward the desk and leaned over the book, being very careful not to touch it.

"Good morning, Lindy," it read.

Lindy looked around, but saw no one. "Good morning?" she replied, feeling a bit silly to be speaking aloud to a book.

"I am Bodleian, the library here in The Crofts," the book wrote, "and you are welcome to borrow whatever books you would like from me, though I do insist that you return them in the same condition that you took them."

Lindy was not certain how to address a library, and she did not want to offend, so she thought it would be best to be as polite as she could. "Thank you very much," she ventured, "I'd love to come and read some time, but I'm actually trying to find the kitchen right now. Do you know where I could find it?"

"Unfortunately," the book replied, "I am not able to move about the house like you are, so I have never been to the kitchens. I fear that my directions would be very bad indeed."

"Thanks anyway," said Lindy, and then paused awkwardly. She really had nothing more to say, but she thought it might be rude just to leave all of a sudden. "Um, well, I should really go and find the kitchen if I can," she said. She felt something like disappointment from the library, though nothing further was written in the book. "I promise that I'll come back as soon as I can," she assured, "and would you mind if I looked around a bit before I went?"

"I would be grateful for your company," the book said, and there was a feeling of pleasure around Lindy now. "Please, take as long as you like."

Lindy said, "Thank you" again, and made her way out through the door once more, still feeling awkward, but feeling too that the library might come to be a friend, so she decided to take a look around like she had promised, just to keep it company. The next door in the hallway was closed, but she opened it and peeked inside. It was almost exactly like the one she had just left, filled with countless books, only it had no fireplace or chair, just a long table against one wall, like a counter. She did not go into this room, but closed it again, and went on to the next and the next. Each one was filled just the same with books, though the furniture was always a bit different from room to room.

Lindy had always loved books. They were easier than people. They were never too loud, and they never asked her for anything, and they always stayed where she put them. She was proud of her own little library of books that people had given her for birthdays and Christmases or that she had bought from garage sales with her allowance, but she had never imagined that someone could own so many books. They made the cozy little rooms feel very safe to Lindy, and she wondered what it would be like to curl up in that old leather chair in front of the fieldstone fireplace and just read forever. If only she could find the way from the library to the kitchen and back, she thought, she would even have someone to feed her, but the thought of food reminded her that she was hungry and that she still had no idea where the kitchen actually was, so she closed the last of the library doors and turned once more to finding her way through the house.

The door at end of the library corridor opened onto a landing with one stairway that led up into the floors above and another that led down below. She was fairly certain that the kitchen was downstairs, and besides, every fairytale that she had ever read had something strange and mysterious living in an attic or an old tower, so she thought it was probably best to follow the stairs downward. The house, however, seemed to be calling her upward instead, and before she had even decided which way to go, she realized that her foot was already on the lowest upward step, and when she had finished wondering how this had happened exactly, she found that she had gone a few steps higher, so she gave up trying to decide anything and let the house lead her up the stairs. After all, Lindy thought, it only made sense that the house would know best about where she was and about how to get her where she needed to go.

The stairs wound continuously upwards, but not in any regular way. Sometimes they went straight, sometimes they curved, and sometimes they turned sharply at landings that had windows overlooking the garden or doors that led onto hallways and rooms. Lindy stopped at each of the doors, and opened them, and looked into them, but she never went through them, though they sometimes looked very interesting. One opened into the balcony of a theatre with a stage and rows of chairs. Another led onto a long windowed hallway that ran along the peak of a roof toward a large dome. Another was mostly windows, and it had a long table shaped like a horseshoe that went all around its edges. Another had a glass ceiling like a green house and was filled with plants and birds and a pond with fish.

Lindy soon realized that she could not really be in Mister Hat's house at all. His house was certainly very large, especially in comparison to her own, but it was not nearly tall enough for such a long staircase, and it was not nearly wide enough to hold such enormous rooms. She also knew that Mister Hat's house did not have a hallway of windows along any of its roof peaks or a tower in the middle of it or a big dome or any of the other things she saw. The house she was in now was clearly not the same house that she had seen so often from her attic window.

Just as she was thinking this, she turned another corner and saw that the stairway ended abruptly at a small door. She stopped for a moment, but then opened the door and peered through it, just as she had with all the others. Instead of a room or a hallway, this last door opened onto another set of stairs, much narrower and much steeper and much more regular than the ones that she had just climbed. Each flight had exactly the same number of steps, and each turned precisely to the right at the landing, so she had the sensation that the staircase would never end. At last, when her legs were beginning to say that they were just about done with all this climbing, the stairs did indeed end above her, not at a regular door in the wall, but at a kind of hole in the floor, like the trapdoor to her attic cubby.

The stairs had been so dim and so plain and so narrow that Lindy was sure she would find an attic with a low ceiling, full of boxes and chests, something like her own. Instead, she found a room that was the biggest and most beautiful that she had seen in the whole house. It was wider and higher even than a theatre, stretching up like the peak of a church to the stained glass windows that ran around the top of the walls and covered the ceiling. The wood of the panelling and the floors was stained in beautiful patterns and perfectly polished. Huge chandeliers hung from the ceiling, already lit, though the sun was only just now beginning to set.

Despite its great size, the room was almost empty. There was a very long fireplace against one wall where a fire was burning low, as if it had been lit several hours before. In front of the fire, though not too close to it, there was also a long wooden table, with carvings on its legs and edges. It stood on a carpet woven of deep blues and bright golds, and it had twelve chairs on either side, with one more chair at the end closest to the fireplace. This chair was turned away from the table toward the fire, and its back was taller than the other chairs, so it took Lindy a moment before she noticed that there was a hand laid on the armrest and a person sitting in the chair.

"Hello Lindy," said a voice from the chair, a stern and a quiet and a gentle voice. "I'm glad I could return in time to meet you here tonight. Things might have been quite different if you had found this room without me."

As the voice was speaking, the person in the chair rose and turned toward Lindy. She knew at once that it was Mister Hat, but it was an altogether different Mister Hat from the one she had followed down the street so often. He was younger and stronger, and he was wearing a long robe of green worked with gold embroidery, and he had a crown of golden leaves in his hair. He was, Lindy recognized, the golden king that she had first seen coming through the arch, and she knew right away that he had always been this king, even when he had walked past her house each day. She felt a strange kind of wondering fear, and she tried to bow like people do in books, only she felt as if someone pushed her just enough to lose her balance, and she stumbled, falling on her knees right there on the hard floor.

— 6 —

In Which Some Mysteries Are Explained

As you might imagine, Lindy was somewhat embarrassed to have stumbled and fallen in front of Mister Hat. She had wanted to meet him for so long, and when she finally got the chance, she had tripped and made a fool of herself. She felt sure that Mister Hat would laugh at her or maybe even be angry, but when she was finally brave enough to look up, he still had the same kingly but gentle look on his face, and he helped her to her feet as if nothing out of the ordinary had happened.

"You probably need to have a seat," he said, taking her hand and leading her to a chair near the head of the table. "I know how long those stairs are. I don't walk them myself anymore, of course," he added, bending down and tapping his knee, "but I remember them all too well," and he smiled a smile that made Lindy feel a little less foolish.

The chair was large enough for Lindy to curl her legs up, and it was warm from the fire too, so it felt quite cozy, even in such a big room. "Thank you... um... Mister Owen," she said, remembering just in time to call Mister Hat by his real name, but then she remembered too that he was actually Mister Bridgebane or something, and then she remembered that he was also some kind of king, so she said, "I mean, thank you, Mister Bridge... ah... your majesty," and she began to feel embarrassed all over again.

"You're very welcome," said Mister Hat, "but only Clinton worries about the formalities around here, so no misters, and no sirs, and no your majestys. Besides, Mister Owen isn't really my name any more than Mister Hat is, not here at The Crofts. Here my name is Alisdair Bridgebane, and everyone calls me Alisdair, so just plain Alisdair will do for you too." He stopped and smiled at her again. "And certainly no bowing or kneeling." Lindy blushed, remembering her fall, but there was something about his smile and his voice that made his teasing gentle.

Mister Hat, or Alisdair, as she guessed she should call him now, sat next to Lindy in the big chair where she had first found him. He settled himself and crossed his legs at the knee. "Would you like some tea?" he asked. "You must be hungry by now."

Lindy was not exactly sure when now was anymore. She certainly was hungry though, so she nodded, and

Mister Hat rang a little golden bell. It made such a quiet chime that Lindy could not imagine how anyone else would hear it, but only a moment later it rang again all by itself, and Mister Hat said, "That's Penates letting us know the food will be up in just a minute. He's probably been waiting for us to ring for ages now."

As he said this, Lindy was suddenly reminded that her mother would probably also be waiting with dinner and would be very worried after all this time. "My Mom..." she started to say, then realized that Mister Hat was still saying something, so she stopped, and then thought that she should apologize, and then realized that she would be interrupting again, so she ended up saying only, "I'm... um..." and then trailing off into nothing.

"Oh, yes, your mother," Alisdair said. "I'm very sorry. I should have told you right away that you don't need to worry. Things are different here. I don't know the why of it, but there's no time in this place, not like you think of it anyway. It's not that time has stopped exactly, or even slowed down. It's more like everything is between one time and another. Your mother will never know you were gone, no matter how long you stay here."

This made Lindy feel a little better, but she was still not quite sure if she understood, and she was just about to ask Alisdair to explain further when Moe came lumbering up the stairs with a tray of food. He looked like Moe the man now rather than Moe the monster, and he smiled his gentle smile as he laid the tea on the table, complete with sourdough biscuits and butter and what looked like homemade currant jam. The food reminded Lindy of how hungry she really was, and she had to make herself wait politely for Alisdair to pour the tea before she buttered herself one of the still-warm biscuits.

"This house isn't the same as the one next to yours," Alisdair continued, passing his hand absently back and forth through the steam of his tea. "It's in the same place, in a way, and it's been there for a very long time, so parts of it have started to look the same, but it's far different from any other house you're likely to see."

He took a sip from his mug. "The house next to yours is actually the house I grew up in. It's called Owen House, because it was built by my family, and it was surrounded by forest then, but you'd have to be as old as I am to remember those days." He looked away to his left, through the wall. "There was forest for miles in that direction," he said. "I used to walk in it almost every day, sometimes right through the place where your yard is now, but that was before the loggers came and before all the houses were built."

The walls of the room seemed to disappear as he talked, and Lindy found herself looking out across her own neighbourhood, with its houses and roads, and the park and the school, and the shops at the corner and the church with the steeple, but it was as if time was running backwards. First the newest houses down the street disappeared, then the streetlights, then the paved roads, and then the older houses, including Lindy's. Where they had been, there were now only farm fields and the railroad track and a narrow dirt road, and then, all at once, even the fields were gone, and trees were growing thickly in every direction.

"This house, the one we're sitting in now," continued Alisdair, "lies in The Weald, which is a world all to itself, and it has been here much longer than I or anyone else can remember." The forest outside changed, became wilder and deeper, and a river appeared where the railroad track and the road had been a moment before. On one side there also appeared the little stone cottages that Lindy had seen when she first came through the arch.

"It was built when this world first came to be," said Alisdair, "though some say that it just grew here, which may also be true. It's called The Crofts, which means The Farms or The Cottages, and it was once the home of Khurshid. He was the first caretaker of The Weald, long before I came here, of course, and he was a splendid king, famous for his wit and charm and beauty. People came from all the worlds to see him, and his court here at The Crofts flourished. But he became proud and thought to rule over other worlds as well, and eventually he betrayed The Weald through his ambition."

"Betrayed?" asked Lindy.

"The story is too long to tell properly right now," said Alisdair, "but, yes, Khurshid betrayed The Weald. He began to use the arch for evil purposes, stirring up war and dissension. So the peoples of all the worlds imprisoned him behind The Weald's great river, and they set twenty-four Keepers to rule in his place." The view through the wall began to widen as he spoke, so that Lindy could now see the whole of the house in the midst of a forest that stretched in every direction, with the river running through the trees from east to west. There was only a single bridge across the river, and Lindy thought that she could see on the far side of it a man who was shining from within, and it seemed to her that he was singing something beautiful and sad and terrible, though she could not hear anything of the song itself.

Alisdair spoke more slowly now, and Lindy heard in his voice the same sadness that she had felt when she was wandering through the empty stone cottages. "The twenty-four of us filled the chairs around this table once, and the house was full of our families and the people who came to live and work here, but Khurshid has one by one destroyed us or lured us to join him, and I am now the last Keeper of The Crofts."

He took the crown from his head and held it in his lap. "So long as one of us remains to wear a Keeper's crown and to renew the veil at the bridge on Midsummer, Khurshid cannot cross the river, but all the other crowns are his now, and when I die, as everyone must eventually die, he and his traitor kings will be free again to claim The Crofts and the arch and to do evil in all the worlds where the arch leads."

Alisdair paused, looking down at the crown in his lap. Lindy felt as though she should say something, but she was not sure that she knew what to say, and she did not want to embarrass herself again, so she just sipped her tea and waited. The view through the walls gradually began to fade, until all Lindy could see was the inside of the room and the last rays of the sun glancing off of the highest windows. The room seemed very quiet and very still, and she was afraid to disturb it, even to get another of the biscuits from the tray.

The light from the fire reflected on the gold and green of Alisdair's face, and Lindy found herself a bit frightened of him again. Though he had been so kind to her, she saw again how kingly and grave he was, and she saw also the sadness that was a part of him and part of the house as well. She was not afraid of Alisdair himself exactly, but she was afraid of his sadness.

"Couldn't you give the crown to someone else before you die?" she heard herself ask, a bit startled at her own voice.

Alisdair looked up, and his golden eyes met Lindy's brown ones, and there was something like laughter in them. "Yes," he said, "I could. And I will if I can, though the choice is not mine to make." He straightened in his chair and placed the crown back on his head, looking younger and stronger again.

"Come," he said. "We've already taken too long with our tea, and I still haven't told you what you need to know most, that you'll need to stay with us here at The Crofts, at least for a while longer. It seems that Khurshid has found a way to enter our world, yours and mine, though I still don't know exactly how, and I can't send you back home until I'm sure everything is safe."

"But I just came through the arch this afternoon," said Lindy, "and I saw you go through before me. Nothing happened to us then."

"I know," said Alisdair. "It was only then that I first felt something wrong in the arch, as if something was pulling at it from our world, stretching it too thin. And then I felt you come into the arch as well, but I couldn't wait. I had to find what was wrong." He looked down at his hands and then back at Lindy. "When I tried to pass back into our world, the pull was so strong that I had to turn back. But when I tried to pass into another of the worlds, everything was as it should be. So I left Clinton to meet you and went through the arch as quickly as I could, to speak with some people who know much more than I do about these things. To see if they could help me."

"Is that why the bird-lady said there was danger, because there was something wrong with the arch?"

Alisdair's face became grave, and he seemed to look off beyond the walls of the house somewhere. "No, no. There's nothing much wrong with the arch. I sent Cleanna and the bird-folk to warn you because I felt some of Khurshid's servants, the traitor kings, cross into The Crofts, but I hadn't yet learned what I needed, so I sent her to warn you all until I could come myself."

Lindy sensed a sudden flash of anger from the house, and she seemed to see three figures appear in the room, tall and kingly like Alisdair, only dim and insubstantial and terrible, the same figures she had seen in Mister Hat's garden. She started back in her chair, and let out a gasp, but the figures were already disappearing, and she realized that they must have been only another vision of the house. "I saw them today in your garden!" she exclaimed.

"Are you sure?" Alisdair asked, leaning forward and looking intently into Lindy's face.

"I'm sure. The house showed them to me, and they were the same."

"Worse and worse," Alisdair said. He looked past Lindy into the room, as if there was someone there who was visible only to him.

"Are they still here now?" Lindy asked.

"No, no." Alisdair's eyes returned to Lindy's, and his voice was full of reassurance. "They fled as soon I returned. But they shouldn't have been able to come here in the first place. They were once Keepers of The Crofts like I am, but they were imprisoned with Khurshid when they swore to serve him. If they have crossed the great river somehow, perhaps Khurshid can now cross it also. And if Khurshid is free to come here to The Crofts, we are all in terrible danger."

— 7 —

In Which A Dinner Is Held And A Decision Is Made

"What will you do?" Lindy asked. There had been a space of quiet as both of them thought about what had just been said.

Alisdair smiled a smile that began very small and little sad but then slowly grew into something truly joyful. "Well, first," he said, his voice as full of joy as his smile, "first, we'll do something beautiful. Tonight, the peoples of all the worlds will gather here, in this room, and it will be an evening like this house hasn't seen in a hundred years, and the decision we make will perhaps be as important as any that has ever been made in The Weald."

He stood and motioned for Lindy to follow. "Come. We have much to do before our guests arrive, and Penates won't be pleased if I'm lazing around when there's work to be done, even if I am a king." Lindy turned to see that what had been a mostly empty room was now full of tables and that there were people going here and there among them, arranging flowers or setting glasses or placing chairs or doing any number of other things. She never actually saw anyone come up the stairs, and there were no other doors to the hall that she could find, but people kept coming and going somehow, appearing and disappearing, mingling around the tables, walking and talking in small groups.

Other than Clinton, who seemed to be supervising the arrangement of the furniture, and Moe, who was setting baskets of bread on the tables, Lindy recognized only Cleanna, the bird-woman who had flown into the kitchen that morning. The others were a bewildering mixture of the common and the strange. There were those who looked like normal people, even if they turned out to be quite different after all, people like Moe and Clinton and Cleanna, but there were also those who looked unlike anything that Lindy had ever seen. She could guess about some of them from her storybooks, like the centaur and the dryad, but there were many that she had never found in any book. There was a tall woman with the head of a white leopard, and there was a bear-like animal with a body all of fire, and there was a huge man with golden eyes and skin like polished ebony, and countless others. Wherever she turned, someone or something new kept appearing or changing or disappearing, and Lindy began to wonder whether anything in the house ever stayed the same for a minute at a time.

Then somebody put a case of small forks in her hands, and she found herself helping to set the tables, joining the chaos of preparations that seemed to be directed by everyone in general and nobody in particular but that was still managing somehow to get things accomplished. Faster than she would have thought possible, the tables had all been set, and the food had all been brought, and the seats had all been filled. Lindy had only just enough time to find her own seat, which Alisdair had kept beside him especially for her, and then everyone began to sing a kind of prayer together. It had many melodies in many languages, but there was still something familiar about it, and by the time it was ending Lindy was almost singing along with a melody of her own.

The lights dimmed as everyone began to eat, and even the fire in the great hearth burned lower, but the softer light was filled with a thousand voices, mingling and joining, rising and receding, like the sound of leaves when the wind is gusting. It seemed as though everyone there had known each other from years before but had not seen each other for a long time, and so they were all trying to catch up with everyone else all at once. It was overwhelming at first, but the talking was so happy and so mixed with laughter that Lindy soon felt quite at home, as if she was sitting with her family for Christmas dinner or Easter breakfast at her Grandfather's house.

The food was all good and simple stuff, and there was so much of it that Lindy knew right away that she would not be able even to try it all. She had some broccoli soup with a thick slice of fresh bread, and then some roast chicken, and mashed potatoes mixed with garlic and chives, and carrots in maple syrup, and green beans with toasted almonds, and then a slice of cake that tasted like orange and nutmeg and cloves.

As she finished her cake, Lindy thought that she was fuller and more contented than she had ever been, and the conversations around her began to sound contented too, slowing and softening as the coffee and the tea were served. Someone brought her a hot chocolate without her even asking. It was very strong and bitter, with the taste of chili peppers in the cocoa, but somehow just what she wanted. She laid her head on her arm and closed her eyes and knew that everything was as it should be. The whole house felt like an old man who has eaten his fill and is now leaning back in his chair to have a chat with an old friend. Everyone, she thought, was satisfied and happy and ready for a nap.

Just as Lindy was about to fall asleep altogether, there was a sudden hush, and the lights began to burn more brightly, and she opened her eyes to see Alisdair standing at the head of the great table with all its empty seats. He bowed to the hall, then sat in his chair and placed his crown on the table before him. There was a moment or so of silence, and the whole hall seemed to be waiting together, and then, one by one, people began to stand and greet the assembly. There did not seem to be any pattern to the speakers that Lindy could see. There was nobody to introduce them. They just stood in their own time, and then they would take on their true forms, and the walls behind them would be filled with the most marvellous sights.

The first speaker was a tiny, old woman with the smoothest hands that Lindy had ever seen, and she became a hummingbird as she spoke, and behind her there appeared plants that floated on the air like lily pads on the water, and tiny birds flitted among them from nest to nest. Lindy could not hear the songs that they were singing, but she knew that the air would be filled with the beating of a thousand small wings, and that the beating of the wings would make a kind of music unlike any that mere throats could make.

The next was a young man, as tall as Moe but broad and stern, and when he stood he became larger still, until his head was among the rafters, and his voice came from every corner of the room. Behind his vast body, vaster mountains appeared, their peaks worked into towers that reached even further skyward, massive and solid and unmovable.

A long-limbed and long-haired man spoke next, his face at once both worn and youthful, and he changed into a centaur, shaggy-hoofed and broadly muscled, as imposing in his way as the giant. The walls behind him became endless forests and plains, one leading to another beneath stars that shone as brightly as lamps in the sky.

One by one, all the guests rose, hundreds in all, and they took their true forms, and they spoke in their true languages, and they showed their true homes. Lindy could not understand their words, but she could understand their meaning, and she was surprised at what they said. She thought that they would speak of Khurshid and what had happened with the arch, but they spoke only greetings, one after the other as the night drew ever closer to day, greetings on behalf of their peoples and on behalf of their worlds, and to Lindy's surprise, she never grew tired of them. They were like a kind of song, soloist after soloist, each taking up the music where the last had left it. The music was not just in the words, though the words were very beautiful. It was also in the people and in their homes and in their greetings, like loved ones long separated and joyfully reunited.

At last, as the first rays of sunshine were glinting off the highest windows, the last speaker finished, and a silence fell over the hall. What would they do now, Lindy wondered. If they had spent this long just greeting each other, how long would it take them to make a decision about something as important as Khurshid and the arch? Would they be here for days?

Then Alisdair stood, and he placed his crown back on his head, and he opened his arms as if inviting the whole of the hall into his embrace. "You are all well greeted," he said, "and I am strengthened by our common will. Tomorrow, I will pass through the arch to earth to see what can be done to undo the work of Khurshid's servants. May the God of heaven and the gods of all the worlds add their blessings to yours."

Lindy could not see how any decision had been made at all, and she was a bit frustrated because everything was so confusing, and she was a bit worried because Alisdair had said that he was going away, and she was a bit disappointed because nobody had said anything about how to get her back home, and all these bits of emotion began to undo the happiness and contentment that she had been feeling during the dinner and the greetings. Though she knew that she was not being quite fair, she began to feel more and more angry as she sat in her chair and waited for someone to take notice of her and tell her what was going on. Everyone else seemed satisfied with what Alisdair had said, exchanging farewells and departing as mysteriously as they had gathered, but Lindy just sat there feeling lonelier and angrier and more sorry for herself.

When the last of the guests had finally left the hall, Alisdair came and took Lindy by the hand, and she let him lead her toward the fireplace. She was hoping that he might explain things to her like he had done before, and she was trying to think what it was that she should ask him first, but before she could ask anything at all, she found that they had suddenly appeared in the hallway that led to her room. She was startled, and she was angry at being startled, and she was more angry because it was just another thing about the house that she could not seem to understand, and she was even more angry because she had been sitting for so long letting herself feel lonely and upset, and so she behaved much more rudely than you or I would have expected from a girl who was usually so polite.

"I want to know what's going on!" she demanded, pulling her hand from Alisdair's and stopping in the hall so that he had to stop himself and turn back to her. "Those people just said 'hello' all night long, and now you're going somewhere, and you're taking me back to my room, but I can't even find my way to the kitchen from there, or even a bathroom, and I don't even know what day it is anymore."

Alisdair looked confused for a moment, as though he had been thinking about something very different, and then he laughed softly. "I'm sorry," he said, and he sounded as if he really was. "I was forgetting that you don't know your way around The Crofts yet." He reached down and took her hand again. "This house doesn't work like other houses, you see. You don't need to know the way to get where you're going. You just have to think about being there, and then you'll be there, around the next corner or through the next door. That's how we came down here from the hall just now. Let me show you."

He opened the door to what should have been her room, but Lindy could see that there was no bed or dresser behind it, no mirror or picture, only the kitchen, just as she had seen it first. Alisdair closed and then opened the door again, so that it led once more into the bedroom that Lindy remembered. She was still not at all sure what he had just done or how he had done it, but he seemed to think that his demonstration had been more than adequate to explain things, and he went on without giving her a chance to ask any more about it.

"As for what day it is," he continued, "I think I've already told you that we're between times here in The Crofts, but a great feast like we had tonight has a strange kind of time all its own. Time waits during a great feast, you might say. It's the only way that people from all the worlds can come together at the same moment. So, in the time of this place, it's really only late evening on the first day you arrived. You came. Then you napped for an hour or so. Then you had tea with me. Then everything paused for the great feast. And now you're going to bed so you can be rested to see me off tomorrow morning. Does that make more sense of things?"

"But when," said Lindy, feeling a little foolish now for her outburst, "did everyone agree that you should go? Nobody said anything about Khurshid or the arch or anything else."

Alisdair smiled. "They didn't need to say anything.

All they had to say was that they would help each other and help me, whatever it was that I decided to do, and that's what they said with their greetings. Some of them might have preferred another plan perhaps, but it wasn't their decision to make. It was mine. Their only decision was either to help me or not."

"But what if you made the wrong decision?"

"Then I'll have made the wrong decision, but any decision might be the wrong one, and no amount of arguing or discussion tonight would have changed that. It was my responsibility to make the decision, and after I asked the advice of some people whose opinions I trust, I made it, right or wrong. The people gathered tonight to say that they would help me, even though they didn't yet know what decision I would make. That was their choice, and I'm very glad to know that they're all supporting me in what I have to do."

Lindy was calmer now, and she was beginning to feel embarrassed about how she had behaved, but there was still so much that was confusing her. "I'm sorry," she said. "It's just that I have no idea what's going on. I mean, you say that you have this thing to do, but nobody says what it is. It's like everyone else knows a secret language, and I'm the only one who doesn't get it."

"I see," said Alisdair. He led Lindy into her bedroom and leaned against the dresser while she sat on the edge of her bed. "Let me try to explain. As you know, several of the traitor kings somehow crossed into our world, into the world that you and I call home. That's what I felt when I returned through the arch this morning, and that's probably how the traitor-kings came into The Crofts after I left." He sighed and stood again and walked to the window. "We're not sure exactly how Khurshid is doing these things, but however it happened, some of the traitor kings are now in our world, and they will be working to free their master, so I must go and prevent them."

"But what about the house? Won't the traitor kings just attack again if you go?"

"Perhaps, though I have my reasons for doubting it. But if they do, we'll be much better prepared. The Crofts is not defenceless when I'm gone, though it's true that we're both stronger when we're together."

"And what if something happens to you?"

"It's always possible that something will happen to us, no matter what we're doing, but this shouldn't keep us from doing what we must. We shouldn't be rash, of course, but neither should we be afraid. We need only do what is asked of us as best we can, even when it might be dangerous." He paused. "Maybe especially then."

Lindy wanted to ask more, but she was suddenly very tired. "Sleep," said Alisdair. "Perhaps what happens tomorrow will explain some things, and you must be awake in time to see it." He bowed a little, just like Mister Hat used to do, and then he closed the door behind him.

64

— 8 —

In Which There Is a Grave Turn of Events

Lindy woke the next morning with the feeling that she had slept exactly the right amount, enough that she was no longer tired but not so much that she was now groggy, and she was sure that the rest of the day would be as perfect as its beginning. You have probably felt this way yourself some morning or another, as if the day has begun so well that you cannot imagine anything going wrong, and I must say that I am very fond of those mornings myself, even if they do not always turn into the perfect days they seem to promise.

Some fresh clothes had been laid out for Lindy on the dresser overnight. They were cut much like her own jeans and t-shirt, only they were made of some homemade cloth and sewn by hand in just her size, and they fit her so well that Lindy wondered whether someone had found the time to make them especially for her. They felt a bit rough on her skin at first, but by the time she had splashed her face in a bowl of water on the washstand and put on her own shoes, she had almost forgotten that they were not her regular clothes, and she set off in search of the kitchen.

Remembering what Alisdair had told her the night before, she tried imagining that she was in the kitchen and then opening the door of her room very quickly, but she was disappointed to find nothing but the hallway. She tried again, and then several times more, but all with the same result, and she was becoming a bit frustrated, so she started walking down the hallway, wondering how long it might take her to find the kitchen on her own and wishing that she could just appear there like Alisdair had showed her. Then, just as she was thinking this, she turned the first corner, and there was the kitchen, though she did not quite know how.

"It was sort of like learning to skate," Lindy told me later. "If I was trying too hard, I just couldn't do it. But as soon as I stopped worrying, it happened all by itself. And pretty soon I could do it whenever I wanted."

Now, I know that Lindy makes this travelling about the house sound easy, but I assure you that it can be a little harder for some people. I have spoken with many who have never been able to get the hang of it, and most people have a good deal of trouble in the beginning. They either try too hard and get nowhere at all, or they panic and start thinking about everything at once and end up in a closet or a bathroom somewhere. So if you ever find yourself in The Crofts, you need not feel ashamed of using your own two feet at first, even if Lindy was able to get the knack of travelling right away.

When she arrived in the kitchen that morning, however, Lindy was less excited at her achievement than she was bewildered by what she saw. She knew that she was definitely in the kitchen, but the room was now entirely empty. There were no stoves, no tables, no pots, no food, nothing but the grey stone oven, huge and empty, and the broad flagstone floor, cleanly swept and bare.

"Where is everything?" Lindy exclaimed, though there was nobody there to hear her.

"Everything is right where I left it," answered the voice of Penates from the middle of the empty room, and then the cook himself appeared from nowhere, already bare-chested in the cool of the morning, and already in the midst of doing something, though Lindy could not see what there was for him to be doing. He was moving slowly at first, but picking up speed, like one of the old steam trains at the railway museum, until he was going as quickly as Lindy had first seen him, darting from one thing to the next, and everywhere he moved things began to appear around him. He moved to an empty wall and pulled at the empty air, and the woodstove leapt into view with the fire alight. He reached above him into nothingness and pulled down a great brass kettle, like a giant fruit from an invisible tree. He pulled flour from cupboards that did not exist until he opened them, poured milk from a milkcan that only appeared when he went to it, and laid everything on a table that seemed to come into existence only because he needed it.

Lindy watched as the kitchen filled around her, and it was like watching a dance, not like a ballet or a ballroom dance, more like the dance at her cousin's wedding the summer before, where there were people playing fiddles and drums and where everyone danced all over the floor and seemed always about to bump into each other but never quite did. Here and there, moving around Penates, Lindy thought that she could see glimpses of the ghostly people who had filled the kitchen the day before, and they seemed to be dancing too. It was beautiful to watch, and Lindy must have stood there for quite some time, because her feet began to hurt her a little.

"Penates," she called, "could you get me a chair to sit on?"

"Just put your hand out where the chair should be," Penates called back, "and it will be there."

"Like the travelling thing?"

Penates shrugged as he stirred something in a big bowl.

Lindy looked behind her where the broad wooden table and its mismatched chairs had been the day before. She started to reach into the empty space, but the thought of something invisible just waiting for her to touch it was a bit unnerving, and she hesitated.

"A chair is never a chair until you sit on it," called Penates from across the room, "so sit on it and make it a chair."

Lindy had never thought of things quite like that before, but it made a strange sort of sense to her. She turned back around and sat without another thought, and she was not at all surprised to find that there was suddenly a stool beneath her and a table stretched out beside her. She felt, for the first time, that maybe she was beginning to understand The Crofts a little.

The house seemed to chuckle at her, and Lindy realized that she could still feel it around her, quieter than the day before but present nonetheless, and it was comforting somehow to know that The Crofts itself was still watching out for her.

Penates soon had a bowl of oatmeal on the table for her, made with big whole oats and chunks of dried apple and cinnamon and brown sugar, and there was apple cider too, and a pot of tea. As soon as she took a bite of the porridge, Lindy knew that this was exactly what she had wanted, and the cider was good too, though she left the tea for the others who were now gathering around the weathered old table.

Moe and Clinton were not among them, and nobody paid much attention to Lindy other than to smile and say "Good morning," so she sat quietly, eating her oatmeal

69

and listening to what the others were saying. Actually, at first she tried not to listen to them, because she thought that it might be eavesdropping, but they were sitting so close that Lindy could hardly block them out, and after a while she gave up trying.

Everyone seemed much more worried than they had been the night before, as if the decision they had made seemed different now that it was morning. They kept starting to say things, and then stopping in the middle of them, and then pausing to look down at their food, and then trying to finish what they had started to say a few minutes earlier.

One of the group was an old man with long white moustaches hanging down over his lip, and he was doing most of the talking. "It's so close to Midsummer," he was saying, as he fed bits of his breakfast to the raven perched on his one shoulder and to the small white owl perched on his other, "and if Alisdair can't return by Midsummer night..."

"But...he'll be back before then...right?" asked a much younger woman, almost a girl. A ghostly doe with golden hooves stood behind her, and her own face had something wild about it as well, as if she was more used to the forest than to the table.

"Oh, Ceryn, I'm sure he will be," said one of the bird women who had arrived through the kitchen windows the day before. "Midsummer is still more than a week away. There's lots of time for Alisdair to do...well...whatever it is that he has to do exactly. He'll be back in time. I know he will." She bent her head and brushed her cheek on her shawl as though preening her feathers.

"I don't doubt that Alisdair will be back as quickly as he can," said the moustached man, "and I agree that he must go." The others nodded. "It's just that this is all happening so close to Midsummer, and if something should happen..." Some of those at the table looked worriedly at each other. "I mean, if he can't meet Khurshid at the bridge to renew the veil..."

"Yes, yes, we know," said the bird-woman nervously, and she made her preening motion again. "Alisdair must meet Khurshid at the bridge on Midsummer Noon or..."

"That's quite enough of this talk," said a woman at the far end of the table. She had been quiet until then, and she spoke quietly, but Lindy thought that she must be someone important because everyone stopped talking and looked down the table to where she was sitting. She had only smooth hollows where her eyes should have been, and symbols like letters from a strange alphabet kept appearing and disappearing on them, sometimes changing so quickly that Lindy could not really see them, and sometimes pausing for a moment or two, just long enough for Lindy to have read them if only she had known what the letters meant.

"We all know that Alisdair must turn Khurshid back at the bridge," said the woman after a moment, "and there's no use in worrying any more about it." She looked at each person in turn. "Either Alisdair will return by Midsummer, or he will not. Either the veil will be renewed for another year, or it will not. It has always been this way. Nothing has changed. So I will hear no more about it."

Lindy would have liked to hear what else the eyeless woman had to say, but Cleanna sat down beside her just then, and without invitation the bird-woman began talking very quickly in a high sing-song kind of voice. She told Lindy how happy she was to meet her, and said that it was nice to talk with her now that circumstances were less stressful than the previous afternoon, and confided that she had been quite worried Alisdair would be detained longer than he had been, which would have left The Crofts practically undefended, and then she finished by assuring Lindy that everything would turn out for the best now that Alisdair had things well in hand. She said all of this so quickly that Lindy had trouble following, but it was nice not having to say anything in reply, so Lindy just listened, even when there were things that she did not quite understand.

Just as Cleanna seemed to be slowing in her conversation, Moe and Clinton appeared with Alisdair right behind them, and at once everyone was hurrying to eat their last few mouthfuls of breakfast and taking their dishes to the sinks and refilling their mugs with tea or coffee. Alisdair crossed the kitchen, which had become very quiet and solemn, like Lindy's class right before a big test, and then everyone followed him out the kitchen's side door, through the mudroom where Lindy had first entered the house, and out into the garden.

It was a beautiful morning, a little cool and a little damp from the dew, but with a bright sun that promised an afternoon warm and dry enough to put a blanket on the lawn. Lindy felt once again that the day was good, and she wanted to whistle or sing to herself, only everyone else seemed very somber, so she kept her happiness to herself. She walked with the others through the trees, the long grass brushing wetly against her legs, until they all came to the low platform of pink stone where the arch stood. Everyone else stopped then, but Alisdair stepped onto the platform and went to the arch. He placed a hand on one of its pillars and turned for a moment to wave at them. "Don't worry," he called. "I'll return soon enough." Then Lindy had just enough time to remember how the arch had felt beneath her own hands before he passed through the swirling grey and disappeared.

Lindy did not turn away for a long while. Alisdair's going had happened so quickly, so suddenly. She felt as though it should have taken longer somehow, that he should have said something more, or that people should have had a chance to say goodbye to him, but he had gone without hardly a word.

She kept looking at the picture the arch held now, the reverse of the one that she had seen so often from her place on the wall. It was exactly her place on the wall that the arch was framing for her now, only it was not really her place any longer. There was only forest there where her house and her cubby and her mother should have been. She felt very lonely and very far from home, and she wished that she had been able to go with Alisdair, no matter how dangerous it might have been. The day was still beautiful, but she was now as solemn as everyone else.

She looked up to see that most of the others had left. Only Moe had stayed, shuffling back and forth in his baggy clothes. "How long will it be until he comes back?" she asked.

Moe shrugged his huge shoulders. "It's hard to say about things like that here. It could be a minute, or maybe an hour, or a day, or a week. Time here isn't really time at all, so there's no way to tell."

"I feel like I'm going to cry," she said. She felt silly saying it, but it was true.

"No shame in that," the big man replied, and he patted her back clumsily. "We've all shed our share of tears. Just can't let them keep us from doing what needs to be done, that's all."

Lindy nodded, but she had no idea what it was that needed doing, and she could not seem to cry anyway.

Just then, there was a kind of humming sound, and Lindy turned to see the arch filled with silver and grey again, only it was flickering now. One moment she could almost see the flecks of golden stars from where she stood, and the next moment there was only the garden wall and the green of the trees. She thought that she could hear Alisdair saying something, but she could not make out what it was because there were so many other voices shouting over everything, and she saw what she thought was Alisdair's face as well, but it was as if she was seeing it in a pond when the wind makes the water ripple. The only thing that she could make out clearly was the voice of The Crofts itself, and it was crying, wailing and weeping and shrieking, and Lindy could feel the fear of the house over everything.

She tried to go to the arch, but Moe grabbed her hand and held her back. The noise kept growing louder, and the wailing of The Crofts grew louder too, until Lindy could feel the ground shaking and see the leaves on the trees trembling. A kind of shaking feeling began to rise inside her too, stronger and stronger, and then she was suddenly back in Mister Hat's garden. She could still feel Moe holding her shoulders, so she knew that she had not really left The Crofts, but the cottages and everything else, even Moe, had disappeared from sight, and instead she saw Alisdair kneeling on the other side of the arch. Behind him, holding him down and pinning his arms behind his back, were the three figures that Lindy had seen just before she first went through the arch. She knew now that they were Khurshid's traitor-kings, and from the way they looked up at her, she also knew that they had seen her.

One of them, a squat man with protruding teeth like tusks began coming toward her, a broad knife in his hand.

"Go back, Lindy!" Alisdair cried, and in the same instant, he twisted swiftly, breaking free of his captors for a moment, just long enough to take the crown from his head and to hurl it into the arch, which swirled with its greys and blues and took the crown into its depths. "Lindy must wear the crown," he called after it, his voice full of urgency, "Lindy must wear the crown!"

One of the traitor-kings struck Alisdair across the head, and Lindy instinctively stepped toward him, but the shaking feeling returned, and she found the garden drifting away from her. She tried to resist it, but there was nothing she could do, and she soon found herself back in The Crofts beside Moe. Her last sight was of Alisdair lying crumpled on the ground.

She looked up to where Moe still stood beside her, his hand on her shoulders. Others were now running to the arch from the house, and a few of the bird women in their animal shapes were circling above. The humming sound was even louder now, so loud that Lindy thought her ears would burst, and still it grew. Then all it once it stopped, and the silver-grey of the arch stopped flickering, and everything seemed very still, and the only sound was The Crofts softly moaning like wind in the trees.

Then Lindy seemed to see someone in the arch. She thought that it might be Alisdair, but he was blurry, and she could not tell for sure. The voice that began speaking was certainly Alisdair's voice though, even if he seemed to be calling from a long way away. "Lindy must wear the crown," he said, and then again, "Lindy must wear the crown," as if he was afraid that they might not hear him. Then the face disappeared, and Alisdair's crown came tumbling through the blue and silver and grey and fell onto the shell-pink stone. It made a dull ringing sound, like a cast iron pan falling onto the floor, and it was loud in the quiet of the garden.

Nobody seemed to know what to do, standing still in their places, and Lindy found that she was truly frightened for the first time that she had come over Mister Hat's wall. She felt as though everyone was waiting for her to do something, but she knew that she would never be able to walk over to the crown and pick it up by herself, so she stood there with everyone else, not saying a word.

At last, after a time that could not have been nearly as long as it felt, Clinton straightened his jacket and began slowly to walk from the group of onlookers to the middle of the stone dais. He bent down, picked up the crown, and held it above his head for everyone else to see. "You must all agree," he said, his voice softer than usual, but still firm and precise, "that Mister Bridgebane has made his wishes clear, and that the force of necessity affirms his judgement in every respect. Someone must wear the crown on Midsummer's Feast, and Lindy is the only one among us of Alisdair's race. She must wear the crown."

77

None of the others said anything in reply, and Clinton said nothing more, but The Crofts began its wailing again, and its voice was full of anger, growing angrier as Clinton began walking toward Lindy. It was saying no words that Lindy could understand, but she knew it meant, "Stop! She must not wear the crown. She will be the end of everything." Its voice was so loud in her mind, and its anger was so strong, that Lindy was sure everyone else could hear it also, and she wanted to run, but her feet were fixed, and all she could do was sink to her knees as Clinton set Alisdair's crown on her frightened head.

At that moment, as the heavy crown bowed her forehead, everything began to dissolve, and the garden disappeared from around her, and Lindy was surrounded by nothing but darkness and cold, her back against a hard, damp wall. The house at last was silent.

— 9 —

In Which Lindy Makes A Decision

The place where Lindy found herself was very dark. It smelled of damp and mould and rotting things, like the crawlspace under the house across the street where only the bravest of the children would go when they played hide and seek. She could hear water splashing whenever she moved her feet, as if the whole room was filled with a thin puddle, but the only other sounds were the whispering of her breath and the creaking of the house and the scurrying of small feet. Even the house was quiet now, and Lindy was so frightened that she began to cry.

Now, I have said at least once before that Lindy was a brave girl, and I have said this because there was truly nothing much that frightened her. She was not at all afraid of the dark, for instance, and not afraid of small spaces. She was not even afraid of bugs or mice or rats or snakes or things like that, so long as there were not too many of them at once. But now she had to endure all these things together, and she had to face them alone without any idea of where she was or if she would ever find her way home, so it is no wonder that she was afraid, and I hope that you will forgive her for it, because I know that you and I have sometimes been frightened over a great deal less.

In any case, she stood there crying for a very long time, and the longer she was in the cold and the damp and the dark, the more frightened she became, and the harder she cried, and the more panicked she grew, and then she found that she was running along the wall, or at least stumbling along it as fast as she could manage on the slippery and uneven floor, and then she caught her toe on something and fell and scraped both her hands on the worn stone of the floor, and then she started to cry like she never had before.

When she had finally cried all the tears that she had to cry and had begun to think about things a little more calmly, she found that she was half-lying against a damp and uneven wall and half-sitting on a wet and uneven floor. She began brushing her hair back from where it had fallen onto her face, which she thought was the best way to start pulling herself together, but her hands soon discovered that Alisdair's crown still sat on her head, though it seemed to weigh nothing now. She took it carefully in her hands and set it in her lap. It grew heavy again the moment it left her head, and there was a comfort in its warm weight. Her fear and panic vanished all at once, and she sat, cold and wet and hungry, waiting for whatever it was that would happen next.

As if The Crofts had been waiting for just this moment, it suddenly filled her mind again, and Lindy could feel its pain and fear and anger. "So you've finally stopped your blubbering?" it asked, and there was a harshness in its voice that Lindy had never heard before. "It never becomes a Queen to blubber."

The Crofts sounded so full of disdain that Lindy could hardly believe how comforting it had been to her only a few hours earlier, and she had to stop herself from crying again. "Why are you so angry?" she cried. "I didn't do anything."

The house laughed sadly, but it seemed more resigned than angry now. "Maybe not, but you will certainly have to do something at Midsummer, and you will fail, and Khurshid will claim me, and I will become an evil thing, twisted and foul."

"I don't understand. What do I have to do with Khurshid?"

"Do you know where you are?" The Crofts demanded, ignoring her question. "You're in what was once one of my most beautiful rooms, the map room. I took it into me from one of the Keepers, but it has fallen now, as the Keeper from whom I drew it has also fallen, and it is now beyond my power or anyone else's to recover it." The house paused, and Lindy felt its sadness deepening.

81

"There are countless more like it. Would you like to see them?"

Lindy started to say that she would rather not, but she was already sitting against a very different wall in a very different room, with jagged holes in its plaster and with cobwebs on its furniture and with dust lying thickly on its floors. "This," said the house, "was Keeper Aulden's study. Countless people came from among the worlds to sit here and listen to his wisdom, until Khurshid struck him down at the bridge, and everything that Aulden gave me began to fall into ruin."

The room changed again, becoming darker and filled with a smell like rot. Eyes opened in its corners, and small creeping creatures began working stealthily toward Lindy across the garbage strewn floor. She shrieked and scrambled to her feet, but the house seemed unconcerned by her fright. "This was the old chemistry laboratory," it said, "a place of great learning and discovery, the pride of Keeper Dennison until she chose to give her crown to Khurshid. Now it's full of unspeakable things." The lizard creatures had come almost to Lindy's feet now, their tongues flicking out across small, pointed teeth, and the smell of rot came wafting from their mouths. Lindy knew with a frightening certainty that even the slightest scratch by those teeth would kill her, and she knew too that she had no way to escape. "Please!" she screamed, and she closed her eyes, fully expecting to feel teeth in her flesh at any moment, but suddenly the smell was gone.

She opened her eyes to see that she was now in a long panelled room, littered with debris and pitted on its walls and floors and ceilings, as if it had suffered a terrific explosion. Lindy was so frightened from the creatures in the previous room and so confused by everything that The Crofts was saying and showing that she felt sick to her stomach, as if she had been on one of the big rides at the amusement park after eating too much candy. She tried to clear her mind, but everything was too overwhelming. Her whole body wanted to be sick, or to run away, or just to lie down and sleep. "This was the sculpture gallery," the house said, breaking into her mind with its sad, lost voice. "Keeper Woods once. . ."

"Stop!" Lindy cried. She felt as though she would begin to scream or vomit or even cry again if The Crofts said another word about the broken and rotting rooms. "I didn't do any of this," she pleaded. "It's not my fault. Why are you showing these things to me?"

"Because," said The Crofts, quietly now, but full of a fierce anger, "you need to know that I was once much more than I am now. I grew glorious from the homes of the twenty-four Keepers, drawing into myself what was best in them, and I became a house that was truly fit for kings. But all the Keepers who were killed by Khurshid's sword left their rooms to fall into decay, and all who were seduced by Khurshid's promises allowed theirs to become something far worse than decayed, and sometimes the rooms have even fallen away from me altogether, so I am a fraction of what I was, a husk, full of rot and maggots.

"I still don't understand what this has to do to me."

"Then listen more and question less." Lindy found that she was now standing on the peak of the tallest tower, looking down across the house as the wind whipped around her face, and she knew that only The Crofts was keeping her from falling to her death. "Alisdair was the last of the Keepers," it said, "the last of the Crowned, and his will was a strong will, so he and I and Penates and Bodleian, we strove to hold together much that was good in me, the libraries and the kitchens and the cottages and the great hall and much else that you have not yet seen, or these too would have fallen into decay. I was broken, but because of Alisdair's strength, I was not breaking further. And now he is gone."

The house paused, but Lindy said nothing.

"You are now the sole remaining Keeper. Alisdair granted you his crown because there was no other choice, because his crown was the crown of your world and must be worn by someone of your race. So now it is you who must turn Khurshid back at the bridge on Midsummer, and you will most certainly fail, for you lack the strength of will to resist him, and so I will fall to Khurshid. And even if you somehow succeed, I will still diminish, become smaller and darker, more ruinous and more haunted. You lack the will to hold me to myself, and you lack the memory of how I once was. Perhaps Penates will be able to keep the kitchens as they were, and Bodleian may keep the libraries, but all else will fall into ruin, and all that will remain of me is what you have added from your own poor house."

The house laughed mournfully. "Would you like to see what would become of me?"

Before she could answer Lindy found herself in her very own cubby, with her books, and her radio, and the old Christmas decorations, only she knew right away that it was not really her cubby. The window looked out onto the trees of The Weald now, not onto Mister Hat's yard, and she knew that her own cubby in her own house was still far away. She did not cry again, but she wished that she could.

The house left her alone then, and everything was very quiet, like in her real cubby at home. She sat on the old couch cushions with the orange fringes, turned her back to the window, and pulled her sleeping bag up over her legs. Then she took her crown off again, which had somehow found its way back to her head, and she laid it in her lap and tried to think what to do.

As she was sitting there, propped in the comfort of her cubby, a strange sensation began creeping over her, as if she was no longer entirely awake but not yet entirely asleep, and it seemed to her that she began drifting through the attic window, out across the huge bulk of The Crofts, and over the fields of The Weald, until she came to the bridge that crossed the great river. She hung there for a moment, and she could see a shining figure far below her walking along the stream, the same figure she had seen when Alisdair had been talking to her in the great hall, only now she could hear what he was singing, a strange song, a mixture of defiance and despair. Then she was moving again, over the tops of the trees, following the path that led away from the bridge, and she flew for what seemed like miles and miles, until there arose a tremendously tall and peculiar tree beside the path, its leaves shimmering gold-green in the sun, taller and brighter than any other in the forest. Lindy paused again in her flight, hovering above the tree, and then swooped down through the forest to her left, weaving her way through the trees, until the trees came to a sudden end, and a small clearing opened in front of her with a stone cottage in its very centre. Lindy began to settle toward the front door of the cottage, and she was filled with an overwhelming need to know what was inside it, but her dreaming ended just then, and she was back sitting in her cubby once more, and she knew now what she had to do.

— 10 —

In Which There Are Preparations for a Journey

Now, you may think that Lindy was being a bit foolish when she decided to go and look for the cottage in the clearing just because she had a dream about it. After all, she would be going all by herself across the bridge into Khurshid's forest in order to find a place that she had seen only in a dream and knew almost nothing about.

You should remember though that people often do strange things when they feel that there is no other choice, and this is just how Lindy was feeling at that moment. She was in a strange place with no one she knew for company and no way to find her way home. Alisdair had left her and was maybe even dead for all she knew. Even the house, which had been so comforting to her at first, had now turned against her. Besides, her dream had seemed so clear, and her mind was made up now, and nothing was going to keep her from going, not even the most reasonable objections, like how she would find the cottage, or where she would get food to eat, or what she would do if she should happen to meet Khurshid along her way.

She probably would have set off right away, in fact, but she was not so rash as to leave without at least some food and supplies, and she realized that it would be difficult to find anything without causing suspicion, even if The Crofts had not discovered her intentions already. She decided that it might be worth the risk of going to the kitchen, just to see what she could find, but first she looked around for anything useful to take with her from the attic. There was the flashlight that she kept for reading when it got too dark, though she remembered that the batteries were low, and there were no extras to be found. There was also a hooded sweatshirt and some blankets that she kept there for when it got cold. She had nothing handy to carry them, but then she saw her father's old army dufflebag, and she dumped his clothes out of it to make room for her things. She also found some of her own clothes. They were summer things that had been packed away for the winter and would probably not be warm enough for a journey outdoors in the spring, especially at night, but she packed two pairs of jean shorts and a few of her warmer shirts anyway, just in case.

The dufflebag was much too big for her. She had to

cinch up the strap as far as it would go just to pick it up, and she could tell that it would soon be uncomfortable on her shoulder, but she thought it would be manageable so long as she took lots of breaks. She only wished now that there had been some food in the attic, but there was only her empty water bottle, though she decided now to add that to her pack as well. It was only as she was about to leave that she remembered the candy canes that would be in with the Christmas decorations, so she pulled open the box and found a dozen or so of the candies. They were probably several years old and very stale, but they would be better than nothing, and Lindy felt better when they were safely packed with the other things in her bag.

She was just about to leave for a second time, and feeling a little sad to be going away from her cubby so soon, even if it was not the real one, when Moe suddenly appeared right in front of her. Lindy was so startled that she jumped and stumbled backward over a box full of old encyclopedias.

"Oh," said Moe, who seemed almost as startled as she was, "I'm sorry, Miss Lindy, for surprising you like that, and uninvited too, I know. But Penates said you might be needing someone to talk to, and you were gone such a long time, so I thought I'd come and see if you were alright." He reached down and lifted Lindy to her feet as he was saying this and then noticed the bag still dangling from her shoulder.

"Miss, Lindy!" he cried, changing to his more monstrous self, startling Lindy once again. "You're not leaving are you?"

"I have to, Moe," Lindy said quietly. She looked down to avoid his eyes. "I can't stay here anymore because the house is angry with me, and I can't go home because the arch is broken, and I..."

"How do you know that the house is angry with you?"

"Because it's showed me all these broken rooms, and it said that the house would die because I couldn't be a good enough Queen..."

"Well," said Moe, looking at her with his big amphibian eyes, "if you can't stay, and you can't go home, where will you go?"

"I had a dream..." began Lindy, and then trailed off, because it sounded silly even to her.

"A dream?" prodded Moe.

"Well, I was awake, sort of, so maybe it wasn't really a dream."

"A vision then."

"Something like that, I guess, and there was a cottage across the bridge, past a tall tree with leaves that looked like gold, and I have to go there. I don't know why, but I have to."

Lindy stood there and waited for Moe to tell her that she was being foolish to leave and that she would be staying right where she was, but he only looked thoughtful and began slowly turning back into Moe the man. "Well," he said at last, "I think, under the circumstances and all, it might be good to talk with Penates a bit. He's the one who would know best now that Alisdair is gone."

He looked saddened, then gave a sigh so big it seemed almost a roar. "I don't know what we'll do without him," he said. "It makes me cry just thinking of him."

He rubbed at his nose a bit and sighed again, more quietly this time, then reached out his hand. "Well, pick up your bag, Miss Lindy, and let's be off to the kitchens. At least it'll be doing something worth doing instead of crying over things we can't change."

His hand was warm and strong, and Lindy could almost believe that things had taken a turn for the better after all as they stepped through the door of her cubby and travelled to the kitchen. She held onto Moe's hand even after they arrived, and he did not try to take it from her, so she took it in her other hand also, laying her cheek on his arm.

Penates was basting something in one of the ovens, but he seemed to feel them arrive and looked up at them immediately. His face was very grim, and even his movements about the kitchen seemed abrupt and angry. He finished what he was doing at last and came to them, putting his hand on Lindy's cheek with surprising gentleness.

"I'm sorry for what The Crofts did to you this morning," he said, his voice still gruff but gentle too. "I hope you weren't too badly frightened."

Lindy was surprised. "How do you know what happened?"

"Because I'm part of the house in a way. The Crofts is the spirit of the house, but I'm the spirit of the hearthstone. We're connected. The Crofts is far more powerful than I am, of course, and I serve it in a sense, but I'm also a part of it. I can often feel what it's feeling and know what it's doing, especially when it feels very strongly."

Lindy must have looked confused because Penates chuckled at her quietly. "Let me try again," he offered. "When the house was being built, that great slab of stone over there was placed at the foundation of the hearth." He pointed to the massive fireplace and the broad hearthstone that supported it. "I'm the spirit of that stone, or I was before it became a part of the house, and now I've become the spirit of the hearth, the spirit of the kitchen, you might say. I was built into the house, so my spirit is bound to its spirit, and so I can sometimes speak with it and feel what it's feeling."

"So you can talk to it too?" asked Lindy.

"Sure. At least, I can when it wants to talk and when I want to listen." He chuckled again.

"But what if you don't want to listen, or what if you don't want The Crofts to listen to you?"

"You just need to will it. Like when you're travelling through the house, or like when you sat on the chair this morning. Just will The Crofts to stop poking around in your mind, and it'll stop."

"I see," said Lindy. She was thinking how long ago sitting on that chair seemed to her now.

"I don't mean to interrupt," said Moe then, "but I think Miss Lindy has something to say that shouldn't wait much longer if she's to say it all."

"I imagine it has something to do with that great sack over her shoulder," Penates said, and there was a good deal of humour in his voice.

Lindy was afraid that he was making fun of her, but when she looked up at him, he winked solemnly, and she saw that he was listening, so she took a deep breath and told him all about her dream, about how she had been asleep and awake at the same time, and about how she had seen the man singing across the bridge and the tall tree with the golden leaves and the stone cottage in the clearing.

All the while she kept expecting Penates to interrupt and tell her to stop taking a silly dream so seriously, but he just listened, nodding every once and while, and looking at her steadily from underneath his bushy eyebrows. When she finished, still holding onto Moe's hand, he closed his eyes for a minute and was very quiet, almost as if he was saying a prayer.

"Miss Lindy," he said, his eyes still closed, "I think your dream is too important to ignore." He opened his eyes and looked at Lindy intently. "Do you remember when I told you just now that I'm the spirit of the hearthstone and that The Crofts is the spirit of the house?"

93

Lindy nodded.

"Well, there are many such spirits, and The Crofts and I are not the greatest among them by any measure. I am among the oldest of the spirits here, but some of the tree spirits are very powerful in their way, and the river spirit is strong enough to keep the law that binds Khurshid from crossing the bridge. Some of these spirits are good, and some of them are evil, and some of them, like your own spirit, are able to choose between one and the other. But all of these spirits are subject to the ruling spirit of this world. We call this spirit Aigonz, and it sometimes speaks to us through dreams and visions like the one you had."

"So, is Aigonz like God then?"

Penates shook his head. "No. What you call God would be the spirit of everything, of the universe and everything else. Aigonz is just the spirit of this world, of this place here and now."

"So, if this Aigonz is the spirit of this world, then why doesn't he just take care of Khurshid himself? Why does he need to have the Keepers and everything if he's the one in charge?"

"Well, I'm not sure if I'm the one to answer a question like that, but I would say that Aigonz has certain limitations, just like we do. I mean, I can do some amazing things, but only if I'm close to my hearthstone. If I go too far from it, I can't do anything at all. And you can do many things as well, many that I can't do, especially now that you wear the crown of a Keeper, but you're limited by your body and your mind. We all have our limitations. We can only do what we are able."

"Well, if it's Aigonz that gave me this dream, then it means that I should go, right?"

"I think so, but I can't be sure. You can never guarantee these things, and you still need to use your head, no matter what you think you've dreamed."

"I have to go though, Penates. I have to."

"I didn't say you couldn't go. I'm just saying that you shouldn't leave this very moment all by yourself with a few things stuffed into a bag that's far too big for you. Stay here just one more night. Let me pack some food for you, and let Moe put some blankets and some clothes in a pack that you can actually carry."

"And let me come along," added Moe, and the fierceness of his tone suggested that he was not asking her permission.

"Absolutely," Penates agreed, "and I think Cleanna should go with you too. Only Alisdair crosses the bridge anymore, and anyone here old enough to remember Khurshid's country would be much too old to guide you. So a pair of sharp eyes that can fly above the trees and look for this cottage of yours might be the next best thing."

There did not seem to be any arguing with Moe and Penates. They made so much sense, and it was so comforting to know that she would have company on her journey, and Lindy soon found that she had agreed to everything. Moe produced some rucksacks and some bedrolls from somewhere, and Penates set about packing dried fruit, and nuts, and some kind of flat bread, and dried meat, and even a few bars of very dark chocolate. Then Cleanna arrived, wondering why Penates had called her, and everything had to be explained again, though she seemed hardly to listen, agreeing at once to go with them wherever they were going, and flying off in a rush to collect a few things of her own for the journey.

Before Lindy quite knew what was happening, the preparations had all been made, and she found herself curled up in her cubby for the night. She had just enough time to wonder whether she could really go through with her plan before she fell fast asleep, and it seemed only another moment before she woke to see the sun already rising.

— 11 —

In Which Lindy Crosses the Great River

The morning of her journey did not go quite as Lindy had planned. She dressed as quickly as she could, putting on the clothes that she had laid out the night before and brushing her hair in her little mirror. Then she tried travelling to the kitchen to meet the others, only to find that she was unable to get anywhere at all. She tried going through the attic hatch to see if that would help, and she tried traveling to other places like the library and the great hall, but no matter what she tried, she stayed right where she was.

She thought at first that this was her own fault, that she had somehow lost the knack of traveling she had only learned so recently, but the more she tried, the more she felt that she was doing everything as she should, and she began to wonder whether the house itself was keeping her trapped where she was. So, after a few more minutes of trying and failing, she gave up and decided just to walk to the kitchen, assuming that she could somehow find her way and assuming that the house had not locked all the doors as well.

The attic hatch descended into a short and narrow hallway that was lit only by a small window on one side. The door at the other end was faded and chipped, so that Lindy could see its many layers of paint, a light cream colour over yellow over white over pale green. The brass handle, however, was clean and brightly polished and heavily made with an ornately fashioned lock. Lindy turned the handle and pulled, but she knew even before she tried that it would be locked, and she was sure now that it was The Crofts that was keeping her from the kitchen, but she also remembered what Penates had said about using her will when talking with the house, and she decided that she needed to say something in as firm and as adult a way as she could.

"I know it's you, Crofts." she said, not so loudly as to yell but loudly enough to show that she was not frightened. "I know you don't want me to go, but I have to."

"You have no idea what you're doing!" The Crofts shouted. The sensation of the house was suddenly so strong in Lindy's mind that she stumbled back against the wall, but she was determined not to let it bully her.

"Stop yelling at me," she said, trying very hard to keep her voice strong and even, and trying also to use

98

her will to calm The Crofts.

"Your will is nothing compared to mine, girl," the house spat back, but it had already softened its tone somewhat, and Lindy felt more confident again.

"I know you don't think I can be a Keeper," she said, "and I know it seems crazy to go closer to Khurshid, but I have to. My dream said so. And Alisdair said that sometimes you have to make choices, and nobody can make them for you, so that's what I'm doing. I'm making my choice. If you don't let me go, I'll go myself, even if I have to start climbing out the window."

The Crofts seemed to shudder or tremble in Lindy's mind, and the house also shook around her, windows rattling in their casings and dust raining from the cracks in the ceiling "You will lose the crown to Khurshid," it said, more softly now. "You're not strong enough to resist him. I beg you. Don't go. For all our sakes." It had quietened almost to a whisper now, pleading rather than demanding.

Lindy felt a sudden sympathy for the house, but her vision had been so clear, and she had no choice now but to go on. "I won't fail you, Crofts," she said, letting her own voice soften as well. "Just let me go. I'll show you that this is the right thing to do. I promise."

There was a long silence, so long that Lindy wondered whether the house would ever answer at all, but then there was a sound like a sigh in her mind, and The Crofts spoke at last. "Do what you will. I will no longer prevent you. But when this ends in ruin, remember that I forewarned you." Then, in the next moment, Lindy found herself standing in the kitchen.

Everything seemed to be moving in every direction, and nobody bothered to ask Lindy why she was late. She was made to eat a heavy breakfast of eggs and bacon and beans and toast and coffee, which Lindy had never tried before, and then she was helping Cleanna distribute everything between the three packs, the biggest for Moe and the smallest for Lindy herself, and at last Moe was helping her on with her pack, and Penates was giving Moe some final instructions, and all the others were saying goodbye. Even Clinton offered Lindy his hand, though he refrained from giving her a hug, as some of the others did.

The goodbyes took rather longer than anyone thought. and the sun was quite high when Lindy and Moe and Cleanna passed at last through the cloak room and out the side door where Lindy had first come into the house, how many days ago she could not quite remember. The sun had already dried the grass, and the sky was clear and blue, and a warming spring breeze was rustling over everything, and Lindy felt better almost right away.

The path from the side door ran alongside the house until it reached the cobblestones of the driveway that led onto the main road toward the bridge. The road had once been cobbled too, Lindy saw, because the smooth tops of the cobblestones were showing here and there, especially along the wheel ruts, but a layer of earth now covered most of it, and there was mud in all the low lying places where the spring rain had made puddles that were only just now drying.

Each step into the spring morning seemed to Lindy another step away from her worries, and she began to skip, hopping from one cobble to another when there were two close enough together. Cleanna must have been feeling the same because she flung her arms wide and took a hop and a leap and then began to fly, her shawl dissolving into a beating of brown wings. Lindy watched her circle ever higher into the air and wished that she could do the same, to meet the sun part way on its long journey to the earth.

It was only sometime later, when they came over a small rise in the road and the trees ahead parted enough for Lindy to see the bridge arching over the great river, that she remembered just how dangerous a thing she was about to do. The sun did not shine any less brightly, and the breeze did nor blow any less warmly, but Lindy felt colder anyway, and her stomach began to ache like when she was sick with the flu. She looked to Moe and saw that he had changed into his monstrous form, his pack becoming a grotesque hump on his shoulders, and Cleanna had returned to the ground now too, standing in her human form and looking very grim.

None of the three said anything, but they all paused together, and they looked down to the valley and the river and the bridge. There were no trees within a long distance of the river on either side, as if the forest was afraid to come too close to it. There were instead long marsh grasses and bulrushes, still young and green, and here and there glimpses of wild irises testing the new spring warmth.

They turned down the hill toward the river, and the road became ever more muddy and overgrown the closer they came to the bridge, but even from a distance the bridge itself looked as sound and strong as if it had only just been built. There was nothing very fancy about it, just wide blocks of very plain stone, smooth and closely-fitted, without carving or decoration, but it filled their view more and more the closer they came to it, and they all paused again when they reached the foot of the bridge, where the muddy and half-buried cobbles met the crisp smoothness of the dressed stone.

"You'll need to lead us into the bridge, Miss Lindy," said Moe at last. "You're the Keeper. We're under your protection from here on."

Lindy realized all of a sudden that this was true, and panic washed over her in a rush. She had no idea how she could protect anyone from anything, and she was not even really sure what it was that they were facing over there in the forest across the bridge. Anything at all could happen, and she could do nothing about it. She was the one who needed protection, but there was no one else, and there was no use going back now.

She took a step forward, felt the hardness of the bridge on her foot, and then she shivered, as if she had come out of a nice warm lake into a cool breeze. Then the feeling passed, and she stepped forward again, and she felt quite a lot braver. The smoothness of the bridge was good beneath her feet after the ruts and cobbles of the path, and the breeze grew harder and cooler and cleaner as she climbed the broad curve of the bridge. She did not for a moment forget the danger of what she was doing or lose the ache in her stomach, but she felt a bit like she had felt when she first saw the cottages, as if she was exactly where she belonged, no matter how frightened she might be.

The bridge was longer than it looked, and it reached much higher above the river than Lindy expected, curving upward like a great stone hill, so it was only when they began to descend the other side that Lindy saw the figure approaching the bridge from the forest. He was a tall man, golden-haired and lithely muscled and naked, walking toward them with his arms casually swinging at his sides, as if he had merely been taking a walk and happened upon them quite accidentally. The only sign that he had even seen them was that his eyes were looking fixedly toward where they stood on the bridge, never looking to the left or the right, even as he walked along the overgrown road.

Lindy wondered for a moment whether she should stop on the bridge and wait for the man to come to her, but she knew somehow that this was the wrong thing to do, so she kept walking along the bridge, downward now, as firmly and bravely as she could. The slope of the bridge hurried her feet, and the man's ambling pace was much faster than it looked, so they approached each other very quickly. Lindy felt a strange mixture of fear and courage at the same time, as though there were two people inside of her, one terrified to go even a step further, and the other determined to keep going as long as she could. They reached each other at the foot of the bridge, her feet on the last of the broad stones of the bridge itself and his on the last of the overgrown cobbles. He was very tall, and Lindy had to look up to see his face, but he bent down on one knee so that they were face to face, and he smiled warmly at her.

"Hello, Lindy," he said. "I'm Khurshid. Welcome to my country."

"We need to pass," said Lindy, and her voice sounded quite brave, though she had been worried that it would sound as small and as frightened as she felt.

"Certainly, certainly," Khurshid said, as if he were a favourite uncle giving a toy to his niece. His voice was soft and gentle and musical, and Lindy thought that she had never heard anything so beautiful before. "Of course, I must warn you that I'll try every way I can to get that crown from you," Khurshid continued. "It's the last one, you know, and I was so close to having it just the other day, and I do want it so very badly."

"You can't touch her while she wears the crown," Cleanna said, quietly and evenly.

Khurshid's voice hardened. It was still soft and musical but no longer gentle. "You would do better to hold your tongue before your betters, bird-woman," he said, his eyes glancing up past Lindy's shoulder to where Cleanna stood. "Besides," he continued, returning his eyes to meet Lindy's, "it's simply untrue. There's nothing that keeps me from touching you, as long as I intend you no harm." He reached out his hand and brushed Lindy's cheek. She flinched, but his touch was not unpleasant. There was no pain or heat or cold, nothing but the gentle warmth of a human hand. "You see," he said, "I intend you no harm. All I want is your crown, and I'm asking you for it now, so you must answer me. That is how things are done here."

"No," Lindy answered, and she did not have to hesitate. Her voice was still firm and strong.

"Well," said Khurshid, "I see that we must now both play our parts. You will do whatever it is that you think you're doing, which I confess intrigues me very much, and I will try and take the crown from you. Of course, your bird-woman friend is quite right when she says that I cannot harm you unless you challenge me yourself, which would be very unwise, but I assure you that I do not have to touch you to do you harm."

Quickly then, he rose to his feet and turned away from Lindy, and he shimmered in the air, and then it seemed to Lindy that he became a gigantic bull, huge and shaggy like a buffalo, with the wide horns of a longhorn steer, and then it seemed to her that he became a tremendous snake, long as an anaconda and wide as a python, its head reared up much taller even than a grown man, and at last she saw him take the form of a lion, with a heavy golden mane and powerful shoulders and fierce jaws. It roared savagely once and then loped away down the road to the forest, never looking back, leaving Lindy standing on the last stone of the bridge.

— 12 —

In Which a Great Evil Is Done

Lindy waited for a long time before she took the last step from the bridge into Khurshid's lands. First she waited to watch Khurshid disappear into the forest, and then she waited a bit longer to be sure that he was truly gone, and then she waited even a bit longer because it was hard to know when to start. Moe laid his arm on Lindy's shoulder, and Cleanna took Lindy's hand, and she knew that they were both waiting for her, but she still could not make herself take that first step.

It was not that the forest itself looked so frightening. It looked like a perfectly normal forest, just like any other forest she had seen back home, without even the strange sense of rightness that lay over everything at The Crofts. It was just that Lindy had half-expected Khurshid's country to be full of darkness and rottenness, with nasty things living in its shadows, like the things that Bilbo had found in Mirkwood, or like the things that Mole had found in the Wild Wood, but Khurshid's country looked nothing like this. The meadow just before them was like any other spring meadow, full of dry grasses from the year before and green shoots growing up everywhere among them. And the forest looked like any other spring forest, with evergreen trees standing fully clothed in their needles, while everything else was wearing thin new robes of pale green leaves or waiting for their growing buds to cover their bare branches. It all seemed too ordinary, too natural, too beautiful to be the home of something as evil as Khurshid, and it made Lindy feel uncertain.

She knew, though, that she could not stand there forever. She could either go back to The Crofts, which she was sure would be a very cowardly thing to do, or she could go on and try to find the cottage that she had seen in her dream. She already knew what choice she would make, but it was one thing to make the decision and another thing altogether actually to do it. Still, waiting was not going to make it any easier, and the sun was already well past its height, so at last she gathered up her courage, and she stepped onto the cobble stones and began walking toward the forest.

The meadow was broader on Khurshid's side of the river, and the sun was very warm, foretelling the coming summer, but the forest was cool when they reached it, and there were even a few patches of snow in the shade and the hollows of the deepest thickets. Though the forest was mostly quiet, there were often the sounds of songbirds just out of sight, and there were squirrels now and again, and they even saw a long slender grass snake warming itself on a rock where the path let the sun into the canopy. Lindy was never quite able to forget where they were or what Khurshid had said to her, but the forest was so beautiful in the muddy sort of way that forests are beautiful in spring that she found herself enjoying the walk even still.

"I don't understand," she said to Moe and Cleanna after a time. "If Khurshid is so evil, why is his country so beautiful?"

"Not all evil things are ugly, Lindy," replied Cleanna, "and not all good things are beautiful." She gestured toward the forest, "Besides, there's still much goodness here. Evil's greatest frustration is that goodness continues to grow, even where it's least expected. Evil is never able to destroy goodness wholly, and never forever. Goodness always clings on, though sometimes only in the smallest ways."

"So, why," asked Lindy, "is everyone so afraid to come here. It doesn't seem so bad to me."

"Oh, well," said Cleanna, looking a little worried, "there's certainly plenty in the forest to fear, I assure you, and much of it looks as evil as it is. Sometimes beautiful things only hide a deeper ugliness. That's why Khurshid leaves the forest mostly untouched, I think, be-

109

cause it pleases him to see something so beautiful hiding things that are so evil."

Lindy thought about this for a minute, and all three of them were quiet for a long time, just walking the road and feeling the cool of the forest and watching the spots of sunlight trickling through the leaves. Then, just as she was about to say that she might like to stop and have lunch, Lindy saw something moving on the road ahead. It looked like the deer that sometimes appeared at her Grandfather's cottage, only it was much smaller, and when she looked closely she could see others as well, hiding here and there among the trees. She looked over to Moe and Cleanna to tell them what she had seen, but they had already noticed the deer themselves and were watching the creatures as curiously as Lindy was.

The little animals had seen Lindy and the others as well, and they investigated the newcomers to their forest with timid interest. As Cleanna began setting out their lunch, the deer came closer in fits and starts, from tree to tree, until at last they were close enough that Lindy could toss one of them a crust from her bread, and it was not long before all of the deer were crowding around them looking for food. The braver among them came right up to feed from Lindy's hand, while the more timid stayed just beyond her reach, waiting for her to toss something in their direction. Lindy's crusts were gone quite soon, however, and she did not know how long the food would need to last, so she could not afford to feed them anything more. Even so, the deer gave no sign that they would leave, circling Lindy and her companions as they finished their lunch and repacked their things and set off along the road once more.

For a short time the deer even followed after them, running through the trees on either side of the road. Some grew brave enough to run after Lindy's heels, and she would sometimes slow suddenly to watch them skip nimbly around her. After a time, however, the deer slowed and then stopped altogether, as if they had come to some invisible border, and then they disappeared back into the forest, leaving the three travellers alone once again.

The path seemed much more lonely without the little creatures, especially since the sun had started to go down behind the trees. It would be a long time before its light found the horizon and things became truly dark, but Lindy began thinking that it might be time to stop and make what camp they could. She was just about to say so, when she heard Moe behind her saying in his low and gentle voice, "There's a good spot to camp over there, Miss Lindy." He pointed over to their left. "See that grove of trees in the meadow there? That should give us some shelter and let us see if anyone is coming too."

"I'll fly up and have a look around a little," offered Cleanna. "Maybe I can catch sight of the tree where we're supposed to turn." She flapped into her bird form

111

and spiralled swiftly above the canopy, leaving Moe and Lindy to carry the three packs to the grove of trees. It was bigger than it had looked from the path, maybe fifty trees altogether, mostly cedar and something that looked a little but not quite like birch and a few other evergreens too. The litter from the cedars smelled good, and it was soft under Lindy's feet. Moe chose a nice smooth area to set up their camp, and he had a fire burning very quickly from the dead wood under the trees. He went off then to find enough wood to last them the night while Lindy laid out the blankets and set the food for their supper. She could almost imagine that she was camping with her mother like they did every summer, only they had no tents or cook stove or anything like that now, just a few blankets and some cold food.

Moe did not go very far, making sure that he always kept Lindy and the camp in sight, but he soon had quite a lot of wood piled up, all broken into lengths. He was just stacking the last of it when Cleanna came flitting down and settled by the fire.

"I couldn't see anyone around," she said, pulling her shawl around her shoulders and leaning close to the fire. "And I didn't see any trees tall enough to be the one you saw in your dream, Lindy, but I did see some smoke from a fire or a chimney a long way off. I thought about having a look, but it was getting dark, and I didn't want to get lost."

"Do you think it might be the cottage?" asked Lindy.

"It might be. It's on the right side of the road."

Lindy was about to say something more, but just then they all heard footsteps in the leaf litter, and they turned to see Khurshid approaching their camp through the trees. He looked as he had at the bridge, tall and golden-haired and beautiful, and he moved with the same ease, and he was carrying in his arms one of the little deer that had followed them as they walked that afternoon.

"Good evening, Lindy," he said, when he had stepped past the last of the trees and into the circle of flickering light cast by their fire. "You certainly have found a cozy camp for the night. You'll sleep very well, I'm sure."

"What do you want?" demanded Cleanna, her voice shrill and nervous.

"I have warned you about speaking to me, bird-woman," Khurshid said sternly, but losing none of his dignity. He turned back to Lindy. "I only came to let you know," he continued, "that you need to be more careful now in choosing the people and the things you love." He stroked the cheek of the deer he was holding with great gentleness. "You see, I may not be able to harm you, but I'm quite capable of harming other things, like this little fellow here," he said, looking down at the small form in his arms. "Isn't it lovely? So small and innocent. You seemed quite taken with him this afternoon."

Khurshid's eyes met Lindy's just then, and they were full of a terrible joy, and then she saw his free hand seize the deer by the throat and break its neck with a savage

113

twist.

"No!" cried Lindy, and at the same moment Moe lunged forward, already changing into his monstrous self and reaching for Khurshid with his huge webbed hands.

Khurshid batted him aside with an almost casual blow. "That was unwise, my little monstrosity," he said. "Don't you know that the protection of your young Keeper is good only so long as you do me no harm? I could kill you this very moment." He squatted down beside Moe and looked into his eyes. "But I won't," he went on, looking back to Lindy, "as a sign of good faith to you, my dear."

He stood again and walked to Lindy, reaching out to brush her cheek, just as he had brushed it only a few hours earlier at the bridge and just as he had brushed the deer's cheek only a few moments ago. "Remember, I reward as well as I punish. But I can only reward once you give me the crown, and I will never cease punishing until you do." He was still holding the deer by its broken neck, and he threw it now onto Lindy's blankets. "This is what I will do to everything you love. So ask yourself how much sacrifice that crown is really worth to you."

He turned smoothly on his heel, and then he seemed to blend with the last few rays of sunlight, and then he was gone.

— 13 —

In Which All Lindy's Plans Come to Disaster

When Lindy was sure that Khurshid was gone, she took the body of the deer and buried it under some cedar litter and piled some rocks on top of it. She wished that she could have buried it more properly, but the evening was now getting very dark, and they had no shovel for digging, only Moe's knife, so there was nothing more that they could do.

Moe patted Lindy's shoulder as they walked back to the fire and told her that things would be alright, and Cleanna said the same, but Lindy felt anything but alright. She lay down in her blankets and tried to sleep, but she kept thinking of the little deer that had been lying right where she was lying now, and she felt very alone and very frightened and more than a little angry too. She knew, just as you and I do, that it was not really her fault the deer had died. It was Khurshid who had killed it. All she had done was feed it and play with it. But she still felt guilty. After all, if she had never crossed the bridge and had never played with the deer, it would never have been killed. It was not her fault that the deer was dead, but it had died because of her, and she could not stop thinking about it.

She rolled over so that the fire could warm her back, and she saw Cleanna sitting on a fallen log keeping watch. Then she must have slipped into a kind of half-dreaming, because the fire grew impossibly high and bright behind her, and there were shadowy shapes all through the trees as far as she could see, and she saw that Cleanna was gone and that Khurshid was sitting on the log where she had been, and at last she woke to find that Cleanna was indeed gone but that it was Moe who had taken her place and that everything was as peaceful as a forest night can be.

She fell back asleep, more deeply this time, and she did not remember her dreams, though she knew that they must have been unpleasant because she woke all tangled in her blankets, as if she had been running or wrestling in them, and she felt more tired than before she had gone to bed. She was also colder and damper than she could ever remember being. The fire was still burning, but it was low, and its heat could not match the morning cold.

Lindy would have liked a nice bowl of oatmeal and a

cup of hot tea, but there were only apples and bread and water, so it looked like a cold breakfast until Moe had the idea of roasting the apples over the coals of the dying fire. The roasted apples were very hot, and Lindy had burnt her fingers and her tongue before she was done, but she did feel a bit warmer, especially after she drank some of the water that Cleanna had left to heat by the fire while they packed.

Nobody said much as they ate their breakfast and packed their few things. Moe apologized for losing his temper the night before and putting everyone in danger, and Lindy said not to worry about it, and Cleanna said that no one could blame him, and then they all went back to packing their blankets. It looked to be another beautiful day, and Lindy thought that the leaves had opened even more overnight, but the beauty of it all was spoiled by the thought of the small dead creature lying on her blankets the night before. She kept imagining ways that she could have stopped Khurshid, how she might have taken the deer from him while there was still time, or how she might have said something to prevent him, but no amount of imagining could change what had happened, and she was always left with the horrible thought of the strangled animal lying in her bed.

They returned to the main road just as the sun was truly up over the trees, all of them still quietly thinking their separate thoughts. Lindy was feeling more hopeful and more determined as the sun rose, and she had even half-convinced herself that they would be able to find the cottage before nightfall, but her hope and determination lasted only the few hundred yards it took them to come across the first of the dead deer in the road. At first Lindy thought it might be the same one that Khurshid had killed the night before, that he had uncovered it and put it in their path, but when she bent down to it, she could feel that it was still warm, and she knew that it must have been dead only a few minutes. She carried it gently to the edge of the road, trying not to cry, and wondering how much more she could bear.

"We should keep going, Miss Lindy" said Moe, as she began to pile leaves over the body. "We don't have time to do things proper. Just say a prayer, and then we'll have to keep on."

Lindy knew that Moe was right, and she got to her feet again, but she felt like something was breaking inside of her. "It's all my fault," she said.

"No dear," said Cleanna, putting her arm around Lindy's shoulders. "You we're only being kind and gentle with the little creatures, as anyone else would do. It's Khurshid's fault. You can't go blaming yourself for his evil doings."

Lindy did start to cry now. She could no longer stop herself. "But what am I supposed to do? I can't help loving things, and Khurshid says he'll destroy anything I love, just because I love it. How am I supposed to stop loving things."

118

"No, no, Lindy," said Cleanna, her face full of concern, "you must never stop loving, no matter what Khurshid does. If you let him keep you from loving, then you've already become what he wants."

"Oh, Cleanna, I don't know what to do," cried Lindy.

"You just keep doing what you're supposed to do," said Cleanna, "and we'll stay right here with you. That's all that can be done."

Cleanna led Lindy back from the burial mound to the road, and she held her hand as they began again to walk along the cobbles. The sun was golden, and the sky was deeply blue against the green of the spring leaves on the branches that arched over them like a vast hall, but Lindy noticed none of these things, only the broken bodies they kept finding every mile or so, one after the other. She lost count of how many bodies she carried to the edge of the road. It might have been twenty, but the number did not seem to matter much anyway. Each one hurt her as much as the first. She did not have tears enough for all of them, and she soon found that her cheeks were dry, no matter how hard she was weeping in her heart.

At last, though it seemed that the day would go on forever, Moe said that it was time to make camp, and Lindy sat down in the road where she was. They could find no place as comfortable as the grove of the night before, but Moe had seen that the land was rising steadily into a ridge on their left and that it had formed a hollow at one point where they could take some cover from the wind. He left Lindy to make camp while he collected firewood, and Lindy somehow managed to find her feet and to unpack their things while Cleanna went to scout ahead again. It only took a few minutes before the beds were made and a fire was burning, and it was only a few minutes more before Cleanna returned, her wings fluttering into arms with great excitement.

"The smoke is quite close tonight," she exclaimed, "a little less than an hour's walk, I'd guess. And it really is a cottage. I didn't get too close, but I could see that it was a cottage. And I found the tree too, Lindy, when I flew back toward the road. It was huge, and its leaves look like gold in the sunset, just like you said."

Lindy felt a great flush of relief. She had been wondering how much further she could really go, but now it seemed that their journey was closer to its end than she had feared.

"That's great news," said Moe, and he looked relieved as well. He turned a little smile to Lindy. "We're almost there, Miss. Just a bit longer."

"Not that the wretched woman who lives there can help you much, I'm afraid," came Khurshid's now familiar voice.

Lindy looked up at Khurshid's beautiful face, and she saw that he was holding the twisted body of yet another little deer. He knelt and laid it very gently on her newly unrolled blankets and caressed its fur. "I know how much you like to see them properly laid to rest," he said, and

120

his lovely voice was touched with amusement.

Lindy had never felt so angry and so helpless and so guilty. She wanted to cry and to scream and to run, but she could not do all of these things at once, so she just stood there, wishing that she could be anywhere else, but wishing most of all that she could be back home.

Khurshid rose to his feet and came to Lindy, reaching out to brush her cheek again, as he had twice before, and she had the feeling that she was living the same moment again and again, that she would always have to endure that touch again and again, that she would always have to endure little broken bodies on the road again and again.

She met Khurshid's eyes and saw that he was smiling at her sweetly. "No," he said, as if reading her mind, "there will be no more small bodies on the path. You know how things are between us now, and tomorrow we will stop playing with pets and start playing with things that lie a little closer to home." He laid his hand on her shoulder with exaggerated concern. "Have you seen your mother recently, my dear Lindy?"

It took Lindy a moment to realize what Khurshid was saying, but when at last she did, all of the emotion inside her seemed to gather itself into one tremendous scream of anger. "No!" she cried.

"Oh my," said Khurshid, as calmly as ever. "Such an outburst." He turned slightly and beckoned into the deepening darkness among the trees, and Lindy now noticed that Khurshid was not alone. In the shadows behind him she could make out at least three dark figures. One of them stepped forward and gave something to Khurshid before drifting back into the darkness.

"I don't think you've met my associates," Khurshid said. "They were all royalty once, just like you, before they surrendered their crowns to me." He began turning over in is hands whatever it was that the traitor-king had given him. "These three in particular have just returned from your world, dear Lindy, where they have captured our mutual friend Mister Alisdair Bridgebane."

Lindy was trying not to listen, and trying not to think about what he had said earlier about her mother, and trying not to let her anger get the better of her, but she was failing at all of these things.

"You might like to know," Khurshid continued, tossing the little square object in his hands and catching it, "that Alisdair is still alive."

Lindy could hear Moe and Cleanna both inhale sharply behind her.

Khurshid laughed mockingly. "I wouldn't get too excited. He may be alive, but he's very likely wishing he was dead by now, and I will gladly grant his wish as soon as he witnesses me crossing that wretched veil. I only mention it because I thought Miss Lindy should know that her dear mother is not alone in her captivity but has Alisdair to keep her company as she enjoys my hospitality."

He turned just then so that the firelight shone on

the object in his hands, and he opened it so that Lindy could see inside. She recognized at once that it was her mother's wallet, only the picture inside had been changed. Where there should have been a picture of Lindy herself as a little girl, there was now a picture of her mother, bound and gagged and lying on a stone floor. Khurshid kept the wallet open only just long enough for Lindy to see what was in it, and then he flipped it closed again and tossed it contemptuously into the fire.

"So," he said, his voice full of false care, "I wonder what it is that you'll find on the path tomorrow..." But Lindy did not let him finish the sentence. Even as he turned away from her, she felt herself lose control, and there was nothing inside of her but hurt and rage. She bent and took a branch from the fire and rushed at him, striking him with it once across the head and once again across his arm as he turned back to her, but he was prepared for her third blow. He caught the still burning embers of her club, wrested it from her grasp, and tossed it into the forest. There was exultation on his face, and he seemed to hesitate just a little, savouring the moment like a bit of chocolate on his tongue, and then he struck Lindy across the face.

The force of the blow took her off her feet and threw her to the ground, her crown tumbling off as she fell. Her mind refused to focus, and her eyes refused to see, and her body refused to obey, but when at last she was able to look around, Moe was lying crumpled beside the

123

fire as Khurshid's traitor-kings tied his great arms, and Cleanna was nowhere to be seen.

Khurshid was now standing between Lindy and the fire. "You foolish girl," he mocked. "You couldn't resist me even two whole days. Alisdair would have been wiser to die with his crown on his head. Now, I'm afraid, he'll live to see me wear it instead." He stooped and picked up the crown from where it had fallen in the dust, then spun it between his hands and set it on his own head.

"And you may see it too," he continued, "if you live that long. And what a joyful reunion that would be. You and Alisdair and your mother, all together, watching me cross that bridge at last. I can almost imagine the pity he'll have for you, hiding his disappointment in your failure. And just think how guilty you'll feel, standing there, watching his final defeat, awaiting his execution, and all because of you." He laughed a soft and mocking and terrible laugh. Then he turned and began walking away. "Of course," he called back over his shoulder, "you'll need to survive the night first, which will be no easy task I assure you. But I'll be waiting for you at the bridge if you make it, and I'll be sure that Alisdair and your mother live at least that long, so you'll have plenty of motivation to join us. Until then, I hope you enjoy all the pleasures that my country has to offer."

Then the fire went out all at once, and everything was moonless and dark, and Lindy could hear only Khurshid's soft laughter and the rustlings and murmurings of nameless things gathering around her in the shadows of the forest.

— 14 —

In Which Lindy Finds the Cottage After All

Unseen things surged out of the trees, scurrying across Lindy's feet and hands, climbing over her body, flying around her face, crawling into her clothing, and every-where they touched, they bit and stung and scratched. She tried to stand, but something much larger grabbed hold of her leg, and she stumbled back to the ground. She kicked out with her free foot, felt it strike something heavy, and then she was free enough to find her feet, running blindly, brushing at the tiny creatures that were still swarming over her body. The branches of trees tore at her face, and then she collided with something large and covered in fur. She was clubbed to the ground again by a massive paw, and something heavy and hairy and smelling of animal landed on her chest. She turned her face and arms away from the bestial thing, feeling savage teeth tear into her shoulder, and at almost the same instant something raked large claws across her forehead and something grabbed hold of her leg again, and she knew very clearly that she was about to die.

She would remember that moment forever after. It would come to mind at the strangest times, while she was brushing her teeth before bed, or while she was drinking her tea at breakfast, or while she was reading a book in the library. Each time, no matter how many times she remembered it, she always felt the same panic that she had felt that night, a panic that came over her all at once and made time seem to stop moving altogether. It felt as if she might lie there with jaws and teeth and claws and stings piercing her flesh forever, as if there would be no end to the darkness and the pain and the terror.

Then there came a light. It was not really a very bright light, but in the deep darkness it came like a flash of lightening. Lindy's eyes were turned away, so she was not looking directly into it when it appeared, but she was still blinded at first, and then she saw a large wolf-like animal standing over her, though no longer biting her shoulder and already cringing back from the brightness. She could also see cruel looking insects and rodents scurrying off into the shadows, and what looked like a huge and disfigured bear standing at her feet and pawing at its eyes. Soon even the wolf and the bear had fled, growling in pain and frustration, and then Lindy was left alone in

127

a pool of light in the midst of darkness.

She lay there a long time, hardly believing that she was still alive. She could feel stings and bites all over her. There was blood running down her face from the scratches on her head, and her shoulder was beginning to hurt very much indeed. In fact, she told me later that she almost did not get up at all. Every bit of her seemed to hurt, especially her jaw where she had been hit and her shoulder where she had been bitten, and it seemed so much easier just to lay there. It was the light, she said, that finally made her get to her feet, though this is another of those things that I do not myself quite understand. The light never actually moved or spoke or did anything at all, but it somehow coaxed her first to sit and then, though it hurt her arm terribly, to stand. How a light could do this, I have no idea, but neither you nor I were there, so we will just have to take Lindy's word for it.

She eventually found herself standing beneath the light, and she saw that it was actually a creature of some sort, a large insect, something like a beetle. It was glowing brightly, not with the phosphorescent light of a firefly, but with the clear brightness of a full moon, and it was hovering several feet over her head, beating its wings very quickly, like the humming birds that came to the feeder by her back window at home. It had been quite still until Lindy looked at it, but then it started to dip and weave around her, and finally it began slowly drifting away.

Lindy was afraid at first that it was leaving her, and the thought of being left alone in the darkness with the horrible biting and stinging creatures filled her with panic all over again. She began hobbling after the light as fast as her hurting body would let her, and she tried to call out to it as well, but her cheek and her mouth were too swollen. She was following so desperately that she tripped over something in the forest litter and fell onto both knees. Her whole body groaned with pain at the shock, and her mind groaned too, for she was sure that the light would now be too far ahead for her to catch it.

When she looked up, however, the light had not gone but was waiting patiently for her, dipping and flitting above her head. Lindy knew then that it must be leading her somewhere, and it occurred to her that it might be leading her into further danger, but she could not imagine anything more frightening than being left with the creatures the light had chased away, so she pulled herself to her feet and struggled after it, wherever it might be going.

The next few hours were passed in much the same way. The beetle slowly lit the way, and Lindy followed, staggering and even falling now and again, getting back to her feet, and all the while feeling weaker and weaker until she wondered how it was that she kept going at all. The soft, clear light of the beetle did not reach very far into the dark forest, spreading just a little way around her, like a moving streetlight, and Lindy was sure that she could see things in the shadows now and again. Some were tall and hulking and ran on two legs, and others were smaller and leaner and loped along on all fours, and still others flew from branch to branch or circled overhead. She could hear them too, howls and chitters, growls and whines, pants and shrieks, all coming from the forest around her, first here and now there, never in the same place twice, and Lindy knew that they were circling her and waiting only for the light to falter.

At last, when she was sure that she could not go even a minute longer, there was a tremendous noise from all around her, as if each of the creatures that followed her was crying out at the same time, and then she took a few steps more, and she stumbled out from the trees into a small clearing, and there, not more than fifty steps away, was the cottage of her vision, and in the doorway there stood a beautiful girl, not much older than Lindy herself. Lindy tried to make for the cottage and the door and the girl, but her body decided that it had reached safety and needed to go no further. She fell to the ground and lost consciousness.

— 15 —

In Which Lindy Meets the Inhabitant of the Mysterious Cottage

When Lindy woke, she was lying on a bed of straw and wrapped in a heavy patchwork quilt made from fabrics dyed in earthy reds and browns and yellows. It was nicely warm under the blankets and nicely cool on her face where the blankets did not reach, just the way she most liked to wake, and she would have felt quite content if her body did not hurt her so much and if the pain did not then remind her of what had happened the day before.

All in a rush she remembered Khurshid taking the crown and Moe lying crumpled on the ground and the creatures swarming over her in the dark and most of all the picture of her mother, and she began to realize truly what had happened. Her mother had been captured, and

Moe and Cleanna had probably been killed, and she had lost Alisdair's crown to Khurshid, just as The Crofts had said she would. She felt a sudden sadness and guilt. She was sick in her heart, too saddened even to know what to do, and she laid there feeling more and more hopeless and miserable by the moment.

Just then the door to the cottage opened on creaking hinges, and Lindy looked, expecting to see the young girl from the night before. Instead she saw a grown woman who was closer to middle-age than to youth, though she was just as beautiful in her way. The woman met Lindy's eyes and smiled a smile so open and so sincere that Lindy knew immediately that she could be trusted, and there at the woman's feet, following her through the door, was the beetle that had led Lindy home the night before, though it did not seem to be glowing now.

"Good morning, Lindy," said the woman. She was dressed plainly and neatly in what looked like homemade clothes, and there was something so motherly about her that Lindy half expected to see children trailing after her skirts as she came to the bedside. "My name is Amena," she said, laying a hand on Lindy's forehead as if testing for a fever. "I was hoping we would meet under better circumstances, you know, but at least you're here now, and I'll wager you're not so hurt that you won't recover."

Lindy started to thank the woman, only her face was so sore and her mouth was so swollen that she only ended up making a muffled kind of sound and hurting herself

132

even more, and this made her realize again how sorry she really was, and she began to cry.

"Now, now," said Amena. "You'll do no good by getting yourself upset. There will be more than enough time to talk about things when you're strength is back." She took the edge of her heavy wool apron and wiped Lindy's eyes. "The best thing for you right now is to eat what I feed you and sleep when I tell you and heal as quick as you can." She stood and went to the small fireplace on the back wall of the cottage's single room, then ladled something into a wooden bowl and returned to the bedside. The bowl held a clear and wholesome soup with vegetables that Lindy did not recognize, all cut very small and cooked very soft. It was warm and comforting in her belly, though it hurt quite a lot to eat it.

When she had finished the soup, she was pleasantly full, and she thought that she could sleep again. The beetle cuddled in against her feet, buzzing occasionally in a contented sort of way. Amena called the little creature Saffi, and Lindy found his presence strangely comforting. She watched Amena busy herself around the cottage, washing dishes in water that she carried in buckets from outside and heated over the fire, mending some clothes that Lindy recognized as her own, and then preparing some food at the table. Actually, it would be truer to say that she half-watched Amena do these things and half-dozed, all the while wondering things like what had happened to the girl who had been standing in the cottage door the night before and how it was that Amena had known her name. Though she still knew that there were far more important things to worry her, she could not seem to focus on any of them, and she drifted comfortably on the edge of sleep all that afternoon.

Lindy came fully awake only when Amena took the stew from off the fire and began serving it into bowls on the cottage's little wooden table along with some dark bread and two glasses of red wine, one filled almost to the rim and the other just less than half way. Amena did all this across the room with her back turned, so it was only when she came back to the bed that Lindy realized it was not Amena at all but a much older woman. Lindy shrank back in her bed. There was much about the older woman that reminded her of Amena, and she was wearing the same clothes that Amena had been wearing, but she was easily old enough to be Amena's mother.

"Who are you?" asked Lindy, a little frightened and drawing the blankets up around her.

"Oh, Lindy," the woman laughed, and her smile was the same open smile that Amena had smiled that morning to win Lindy's trust. "I'm still the same Amena. I'm just a little older now, and I will be older still by the time you go to sleep tonight."

"But how..." Lindy began.

Amena laughed again. "It's just the way I am. Each day I grow older, from daughter to mother to grandmother, and each morning, at the very first hour, I became a girl again, like I was when you found me last night. Do you remember?"

"Yes," said Lindy" I do remember. There was a beautiful girl standing at the door of the cottage. And that was you?"

"That was me. And I will be the same again not very long from now, when the last hour of night turns to the first hour of morning."

"But why?"

"I told you. It's just the way I am. The way I've always been. And I have been a very long time." She reached out and took Lindy by the hand. "Now," she said, and her tone said that she had changed the topic of conversation. "Enough questions. I think you'll find that you're well enough to get out of bed for a short while, so you can wash your wounds and eat something. This cottage is the kind of place where people heal quickly, and you're healing even more quickly than most."

Lindy allowed herself to be helped to the washstand where Amena had set a basin of water. It was very cold in the warmth of the cabin, but it felt good to wash herself. Her body hurt her much less than she expected, though her shoulder was still very painful and her face looked a horrible mess in the small and cloudy mirror that hung over the washstand, all red scratches and blue bruises.

Amena sat Lindy down in one of the cottage's two rough wooden chairs to change her shoulder dressing.

The wound was quite deep in places, and it was still very much open and bloody, but there did not seem to be any infection, and there was already new pink skin showing at the edges. Amena washed it carefully in salt water and put some kind of salve into it that burned sharply and smelled like vinegar. Then she rebandaged it and helped Lindy dress in her old clothes again. Amena had washed and mended them so well that there were no blood stains to be seen, and the carefully darned tears could hardly be noticed.

It felt good to be back in her old clothes again, and it felt even better to get some food in her stomach. The stew was thick and tasty and filling. Though Lindy was at first sceptical about eating rabbit in a stew or any other way, her hunger soon won her over, and before she realized how quickly she was eating, she was already wiping her bowl with a piece of the heavy, dark bread. She was feeling drowsy again by then, especially once Amena made her drink the half glass of wine. Lindy had sometimes had a sip of her mother's wine, but just a sip, and Amena's wine tasted very strong on her tongue, and it was almost half a glass besides, and Lindy was soon in bed again and sleeping soundly.

She woke only once that night, shortly after midnight, to feel something climbing on her feet. She was startled, and there was a split second when she imagined herself out in the forest being attacked by the night creatures again, but she soon saw that it was only Saffi, making himself a nest in the blankets at her feet. The fire was low in the hearth, and there was little light in the cottage, but when Lindy looked out from her bed, she could see a very young girl, young enough to be Amena's daughter, sitting in one of the wooden chairs and reading something by the firelight. Lindy suddenly felt safe again, maybe for the first time since she had jumped off the wall into Mister Hat's garden. She was asleep again a moment later, and she did not wake until morning.

— 16 —

In Which Amena Offers Some Wise Advice

The next day and the next after that passed in much the same way. Lindy slept most of the time, and she ate the simple, wholesome food that Amena prepared for her, and she healed at a marvellous rate. By the end of the third day, in fact, she was feeling almost completely whole. The stings and bites and scratches were all healed, and there were only scars left to remind her of the deeper scratches on her forehead that were mostly hidden by her hair anyway. The only wound not yet healed was the deep bite in her shoulder, which still caused her some discomfort and which Amena said might never entirely heal.

Lindy did not sleep the whole of the three days, of course. She had enough energy to sit up and talk or to walk around a little, especially on the third day, but Amena was not always available to keep her company. She had a garden to tend, she said, and cows to milk, and eggs to collect, and animals to feed, and snares to check, and wild strawberries to gather, so she only had time to sit with Lindy while preparing their meal or while changing Lindy's dressings. This meant that Lindy was by herself with nothing much to do for hours at a time, and she was very much bored. There was only a single book in the cottage, and it was written in a language that Lindy did not know, with letters that she did not even recognize. She tried to pass the time by sweeping the floor and tidying up the room, but the floor was small and there was not much to tidy, so this did not distract her long, and when she tried to go outside, Amena sent her back in directly. She said that it was best if Lindy stayed out of sight from prying eyes, so Lindy was mostly trapped indoors alone.

This was not actually so bad, though it was not very pleasant at first. The truth is that she needed to think about some things, but they were not exactly comfortable things, and she was trying to ignore them no matter how much they needed to be thought. When she was left alone with nothing to do for hours on end, however, she could hardly avoid them, which is very likely what Amena intended in the first place. Eventually, she found herself asking how it was that she had gotten into such a mess, and how it was that she could have let Khur-

shid take the crown from her, and how it was that her
vision could have led her so wrong, and most of all what
it was that she should do now. This last question was the
most perplexing because it was also the most pressing.
Her mother was being held captive, and Khurshid was
about to cross the bridge into The Weald, but she had
no idea what to do about either of these things. Staying
where she was would not help anything, even if Amena
were to permit it, and The Crofts would certainly not
welcome her back, not after what she had said on the
morning she left, and not after everything that had happened since. Still, there was really nowhere else to go.
She thought about these things for a long time without
coming any closer to an answer, though she felt a bit better anyway, as if just facing her problems and deciding
that she needed to do something had mended her spirits
a little, even if she had not yet determined exactly what
her decision should be.

When Amena came in from the garden that third
afternoon, she let Lindy help prepare their dinner of
roasted vegetables, and she began kneading the bread
that had been rising beside the hearth. "So," she asked,
as if she knew perfectly well what Lindy had been thinking about all that while, "have you decided what you will
do?"

Lindy shrugged and kept chopping the carrots. "I
don't really know," she said. She kept quiet for a moment, but then thought better of it and let everything

out all at once in a rush. "I don't even know why I'm here," she said. "I thought I was supposed to go to your cottage, because the dream told me to, but then everything went wrong, and when I got here it didn't help anything. I mean, you saved my life, and you've been really good to me, but I thought that coming to your cottage would make everything better. I thought that's why I was supposed to come here. But things are even worse now than when I started."

"And just what did you think you would find here?" Amena asked, looking amused. Her sleeves were rolled up past her elbows, and there was flour dusted on her arms.

"I don't know. Answers, I guess." Lindy remembered how clear her vision had seemed. "I was sure it was the right thing to do," she said, "but it all turned out wrong. My mom is captured, and the crown is gone, all because of me."

"Well, things look very bad at the moment, it's true," replied Amena, "but that doesn't mean you didn't do the right thing. Doing what you're supposed to do doesn't guarantee that things will turn out as you want. That isn't why you do the right thing. You do the right thing just because it's the right thing, no matter what happens."

"So how do I even know if it's the right thing to do?"

"Yes, that certainly is the problem," Amena answered. She began shaping the dough into loaves. "Unfortunately, there's no way you can ever really be sure what the right thing is. You can talk with people who might know, with people you trust. You can try to think things through as clearly as possible. You can look back at your own experience. Most importantly, you can listen carefully to what your spirit has heard. But, in the end, you can never be sure, and all you can do is what you feel is best."

Lindy sighed and scraped the chopped carrots into the pan. "And what if your best isn't good enough? Then it's all your fault."

"No, no. It's not all your fault. It's partly your fault, true, but many people had to make decisions along the way in order to get us where we are now, and some of those decisions were made before you were even born. You can only ever be responsible for the decisions that you make yourself."

"So, you're saying that maybe I was supposed to come here, even though all those bad things happened?"

"I don't know. We'll probably never know. All you can know is whether you tried to do what you were asked to do."

"I think I did."

"Then you chose as best you could," said Amena, putting the bread into loaf pans. "You failed, like everyone fails sometimes, but that doesn't mean your choice was wrong, and if you really believe that it was the right choice to make, perhaps you just need to see it through."

142

"But my choice was to come here, and I did see it through. I just don't know where I need to go now."

"Seeing a decision through to its end also means seeing its consequences through to the end. It means taking responsibility for what you decided. It means facing the people who were depending on you, and probably apologizing to them, and then helping them try to fix the problems that you created."

"So I came all this way for nothing? I lost my mom and Alisdair's crown getting here, just so I can turn around and go back with nothing to show for it?"

"Oh, you have more to show for it than you might think. You know now just how terrible a foe we face, and you know also that you have friends in places you might not expect, and you know too what it means to choose and to fail and to learn from your failure, and hopefully you are learning right this moment what it means to face the consequences of your failures."

"What if I fail that too."

"You might. In fact, you probably will in one way or another. But you still need to do it."

"But if I fail, how will I save my mom? How will I stop Khurshid?"

Amena looked Lindy very seriously in the eye, and there was a sadness in her face that Lindy had not seen before. "Maybe no one will stop him," she said. "Maybe he'll cross the bridge and destroy The Crofts despite everything we do."

"But he'll kill my mom, and Alisdair, and Penates, and all those people."

"Maybe, and that would be a most terrible thing, so terrible I can hardly bear to think of it, but it wouldn't be the end of everything. Good is an easy thing to tear down, but it's a very difficult thing to get rid of altogether. I was living here in Khurshid's country long before he chose to betray The Weald, and I lived through the sorrow of losing my friends to him, but I've survived all this time in spite of everything he can do. And you've seen for yourself that there are other things here that aren't evil, like Saffi, like the deer. We couldn't stop Khurshid from betraying us, but we've done our best to do what is good and right despite him. It's not our task to make sure that good triumphs over evil in the world, though we must always strive for this as best we can. Our task is only to make sure that good triumphs over evil in ourselves. That's all we can do."

The vegetables were all peeled and chopped by now, and Amena set the roasting pan in the oven. Then she put the loaf pans beside the oven to let the bread rise again. Lindy watched her wrinkled hands move deftly around the hearth, and she wondered how Amena had kept going so many years, one day after another, planting and growing and tending and gathering all alone. "What keeps you from just giving up and moving somewhere else?" she asked.

Amena looked up from the dishes that she was stacking beside the washstand. "I stay because this is my home," she answered, "and because I couldn't bear to see Khurshid have it, and because, most of all, it's what I know I need to do. It's the right thing for me to do. So I do it."

"But how do you keep Khurshid from just coming in and taking it?"

"Because this is my home, and he has no right to it unless I grant the right to him, just as he had no right to take your crown until you gave him the right."

Lindy thought about this for a moment. "Is it the same for me? Can I keep my home from him? I mean, I don't have a home here exactly, but The Crofts is sort of like my home. Can I keep The Crofts from Khurshid if I go and live there?"

"No. At least not the whole of it. The Crofts is the home of many people, living and dead, and you have as little right to it as Khurshid does, but as a Keeper, some small part of it is yours, and you may be able to keep that small part good and whole."

"Yes," said Lindy, remembering her cubby, "I think I know what part is mine. And I can keep Khurshid from taking it?"

"Certainly, even if all the rest of The Crofts falls into ruin. And Penates can keep the kitchen, and there will be some others also, and a little good will be kept alive in it still, and then who knows what great good may come from it someday."

"Well," said Lindy, and she discovered that she had made up her mind almost without realizing it, "I guess that's what I need to do then. But I'll have to tell The Crofts about everything. It told me this would happen, and I didn't listen."

"Yes, well, admitting when you've made a bad choice is one of the responsibilities of making decisions in the first place. This won't be the last time you make a bad choice, I assure you. So you may as well learn how to face the consequences now."

Something about this made perfect sense to Lindy, and she felt better than she had since before the terrible night in the forest. "You're right," she said. "I'll leave first thing in the morning," but she thought right away of all the creatures hiding in the woods, and she was already afraid of the choice she had made. "Could you come with me?" she asked.

"I would love to, Lindy," said Amena, and the look on her face told Lindy that she meant it, "but I can't leave this place just whenever I choose." Lindy said nothing, but Amena seemed to know what she was thinking. "Don't worry," she added, "I'll send Saffi with you. Only Khurshid himself would dare bother you with Saffi around. The forest creatures will leave you well alone."

They ate supper and went to bed without saying much more to each other, and Lindy fell asleep quickly, her dreams full of things that she could not remember in the morning but that she knew were full of hope.

— 17 —

In Which Lindy Begins The Journey Home

The next morning, when Lindy walked out the cottage door and along the path and into the woods, she had the feeling that she was only just then beginning her real journey. Jumping down from Mister Hat's wall and passing through the arch and finding The Crofts and looking for the cottage and losing the crown to Khurshid all seemed like preparations for the journey that she was about to make now, the journey back home to Clinton and Penates and The Crofts. She had felt this way from the moment she woke, and she had tried to explain it to Amena as best she could as they ate their breakfast of fresh bread and butter and honey with lemon balm tea to wash it all down. Amena had only smiled at her. "Our most important journeys are often our journeys home," she had said, and Lindy felt how true this was now as she began her own journey home.

The Crofts was not her real home, of course. She had only lived there for a few days, three or four, she could not quite remember, but it was the only home that she had in The Weald. It had felt like she belonged there almost right away, and she knew now that it was where she needed to be, no matter how angry the house might be with her. So she was going home now, at least in a way, and she knew somehow, just as Amena had said, that this was her most important journey.

When at last she had said her goodbyes, she followed Saffi from the clearing onto a path so completely overgrown that it hardly seemed worth the name. It went weaving around trees and along ridges and through valleys and yet, in the end, somehow managed to find the main road just when Lindy had begun to wonder whether Saffi was leading her in circles. He bobbed about, ducking and diving and seeming to choose his way at random when the path disappeared, but he always knew his way, and the two of them always found the trail again, and they did eventually come at last to the main road. More importantly, they saw nothing of the fearsome creatures that Lindy now knew were lurking about in the forest, only a few squirrels and a few songbirds now and again, and these were pleasant enough company.

Once they came to the main road, their journey was even less eventful, and I will spend as little time describing it to you as Lindy spent describing it to me. She stopped once to eat some of the food that Amena had sent with her, and she stopped again that night to sleep in a dry cave that Saffi found, but nothing much else happened throughout the day besides putting one foot in front of the other. Even going to sleep that night, which Lindy had thought might be a bit difficult, was easier than she expected. She just laid her head on her pack, pulled her wool blanket over herself, glanced at Saffi keeping guard at the mouth of the cave, and fell asleep straight away, which is more than I can manage myself most nights, even in the comfort and safety of The Crofts.

She woke the next morning to see Saffi still standing guard, and so she began the day feeling as safe and as happy as could be expected, but there was no one really to share her happiness, and she had to make do with talking to Saffi as she ate her breakfast of wild strawberries and bread. She told him about how strange it was to be in a place so unlike her home, and how worried she was about her mother, and how much better she felt now that she was going back to The Crofts. Saffi could say nothing back to her, of course, and she was not really sure how much he could understand anyway, but it made her feel a little less alone to tell him what she was feeling.

They set off again while it was still quite early. The coolness of the morning had woken Lindy before it was even light, and it had not taken very long to eat her simple breakfast, so the sun was only just filtering through the leaves when they reached the main road again. The dew was heavy on everything, and Lindy's pants and shoes were soon wet from the plants that were overgrowing the cobblestones, but the sky was clear, and the sun promised to dry everything before very long. Lindy thought that she should probably reach the bridge before dark if she walked quickly enough, so she set herself a good pace and kept going straight through lunch, eating the last of her wrinkled apples as she walked.

The sun had grown as warm as it had promised by the afternoon, and Lindy began to sweat as she walked. The warmth of the day reminded her that it would not be long until it was really summer, and this made her wonder what day it was and how close it was exactly until Midsummer. She even thought for a moment that it might have passed and that it might be too late to go back to The Crofts. Her sense of time told her that this was not probably true, but she knew that time moved strangely in The Weald, and the trees did now look full enough for Midsummer, so she could not quite put aside the sense that she was running out of time.

She began to walk even faster now, though she was quite tired from walking so far, and she even found herself breaking into a jog at times, her feet starting to run on as fast as her mind. She could only think now of how she might be late and come to The Crofts and find that there was almost nothing left of it. She began imagining

150

the most terrible things, and the worst of it was that she knew these things might really be true or that they might really become true at any moment.

Saffi did not seem to be concerned by any of this. He just kept humming along beside her, matching his speed with hers, but after a time, he too began to act strangely. He would land on the path for a few seconds at a time, keeping very still and seeming to feel for tremors in the ground, or he would sweep up very high above the tree canopy, as if he was looking for something, and all the while his buzzing became agitated and frenzied.

It took only a few minutes more until Lindy too began to hear something now and again. At first it was only faint and muffled and intermittent, sounding like the works of a big factory, only very far away. Then, after a few minutes more, she could hear that the sounds were actually drums beating, and then, when she was closer, she could also hear shouting and singing and growling and roaring and all sorts of other noises. Soon she could also make out the orange light of bonfires mixing with the setting sun through the last of trees, and then, at last, she came upon a great horde of creatures gathered in the meadow before the bridge, all eating and drinking and carousing and dancing and singing and fighting. Most of them looked at least a little human, though they were almost always wrong somehow, either too beautiful or too hideous or too something that Lindy could not quite name but could still feel in her stomach. They all

151

had a sense about them that they did not belong, a sense that they were out of place. Even looking at them made her feel wrong somehow.

Lindy was too surprised by all this to be as frightened as she probably should have been. She just kept walking along the road toward the bridge, right through the middle of the fires and the noise, with Saffi hovering above her like a halo in the deepening evening. Some of the creatures stopped to look at her as she passed, and soon others were looking as well, and before long it seemed as if every eye was on her and that every voice was hushed.

Ahead of her, right in the middle of the path, nearly at the foot of the bridge, there was something like an old fashioned carriage, only it was covered in complicated carvings and painted everywhere in red and gold. Its wheels were huge, twice as tall as Lindy, and it had steps leading up from the ground to a throne that sat high on the bed of the carriage. Khurshid was lounging on the throne and eating something from a golden bowl as Lindy approached, but when she reached the foot of the carriage, he passed the bowl to one of his servants and leapt to his feet with such a show of joy that Lindy knew he could only be mocking her.

"Oh, Lindy," he cried, "I'm so glad you've come to join us in our celebrations." He lowered his voice to a loud whisper, "In fact, I have the most marvellous surprise for you tomorrow night. Do tell me that you'll be there to see it." He moved down the stairs toward her, stepping around a large golden chest that was set in front of his throne like a footstool. It was carved all over with impossible animals and plants, all holding each other in their patterns with teeth and claws and barbs and stings, and Lindy found her eyes strangely drawn to it.

"Ah, yes," Khurshid said, noticing her gaze, "you've seen my chest of crowns. Would you like me to show it to you?"

He took her hand and led her up the first steps of the throne so that he could lift the lid of the golden chest. It was filled to its very brim with crowns, all piled carelessly, as if they had been thrown simply at random. Lindy knew that they must be the crowns of the Keepers, but they were not all the same as she had imagined they would be. Some were simple circles of gold and some worked in ornate patterns, some heavily made and some quite delicate, some very plain and some covered in jewels.

"You recognize this one, I'm sure," Khurshid said. He picked up the crown that Lindy had worn for so short a time and that Alisdair had worn for so long before her. He placed the crown on his own head. "It looks very regal, you must admit," he said, "almost as if it was made for me."

He picked up another and tossed it to Lindy. It was heavier than it looked, and she staggered back under its weight, almost stumbling on the stairs. As soon as she touched it, her mind was filled with the image of a handsome man, his green eyes quiet and grave, his red hair and beard closely cut like fur and shot with grey. "He's dead now," said Khurshid, "that man you're seeing." Lindy now saw the man standing before Khurshid with sword drawn, and then kneeling on the ground with his weapon shattered, and then lying on the ground with his crown fallen beside him.

The image faded as Khurshid took the crown from her and handed her another. It was even heavier and set with three large rubies, and she saw in her mind a woman, dark-haired but light-eyed, and with the sense of something feline about her, something large and carnivorous. "She was one of the wise ones," Khurshid said, and he nodded to the left of the throne. Lindy saw that a small crowd of people were now gathered there, and among them was the same woman, with the same hair and eyes, the same sense of cat-like grace and cruelty. She stared back at Lindy, and Lindy turned her eyes away.

The images from the crowns saddened her. They seemed to say just what Khurshid had said, that her only choice was either to surrender or to die, and a feeling of hopelessness began creeping over her. She found herself wondering whether there was really any point of going back to The Crofts or even of going any further. After all, had Khurshid not already taken all the crowns? What difference would it make if she went back now? She tried to remember why it was that she needed to go back home, but she could think of nothing but the faces she had seen in the crowns, and they threatened to shut out everything else.

It was then, Lindy said, that Saffi saved her for a second time. Whether or not he really knew that she needed saving is a question that neither Lindy nor I can answer, but for whatever reason, whether because he saw Lindy's distress or because of some instinct of his own, Saffi chose just that moment to land on the steps of the carriage and brush up against Lindy's leg, like a cat looking for attention, and Lindy said that it was as if he had shone his light right into her heart. In that soft, clean light everything became much clearer again. She suddenly saw how Khurshid was using the crowns to drive her into hopelessness, and she saw too that going back to The Crofts was exactly what she needed to do, whatever else might happen.

She handed the crown back to Khurshid and straightened herself up as tall as she could. "That's enough," she said.

Khurshid met her eyes with a look of surprise.

Lindy held his gaze for a moment, then she turned and descended the stairs with Saffi once again flying close beside her. She rounded the edge of the carriage, past its huge wheels, between the traitor-kings who had gathered beside it, and onward toward the bridge. No one tried to stop her. They only followed her with their eyes, and Lindy was already beyond them before she heard Khurshid calling after her from the height of his throne.

"Until tomorrow, Lindy," he cried, his melodious voice singing out into the coming night.

Lindy neither turned nor answered, only stepped from the path onto the bridge and kept her course for home, even as the sounds of Khurshid's camp swelled once more behind her, growing fuller and louder with every step, until she reached the forest and found it echoing again with the sounds of distant shouts and drums.

— 18 —

In Which There Is a Homecoming of Sorts

The night had become quite cold by the time Lindy left the noise of Khurshid's camp behind her. The sky was high and clear, and the day's warmth had fled as quickly as the sun, and Lindy was soon feeling the chill even through the wool sweater that Amena had given her for the journey. It was one of those spring nights where winter seems to return again. The temperature fell well below zero, and a cold wind picked up along the road, and Lindy's breath was making puffs of white in the halo of light that Saffi was casting around her.

She tried to remember how long it had taken to walk with Moe and Cleanna from the house to the bridge all those mornings ago when they had set out in search of the cottage. She knew that they had started later than they wanted and that they had reached the bridge when the sun was still very high, so she guessed it was not more than two or three hours walk now to The Crofts, but the journey seemed much harder on the way back. The road rose steadily up from the river, and she was tired from her long journey, and the darkness made her walk more carefully, even with Saffi giving what light he could.

She kept plodding along the path, not wanting to make camp on such a cold night, especially when she was now so close to The Crofts. She was shivering quite a lot, hugging her arms around herself against the cold and pulling her sweater up around her face, even wearing the blanket from her pack over her shoulders like a cape. None of this seemed to help much though. She was still cold through her many layers, and she was still so very tired. She could not remember having ever been so tired. Her feet were sore from the hard pace she had set all day, and they kept catching on the cobbles as she dragged them one after the other. It was as if she had spent the last of her energy walking away from Khurshid at the bridge and now had nothing left. She kept promising herself that she would be able to see the lights of The Crofts over the next rise or around the next corner, but she was disappointed each time, and she began to wonder whether she might have to stop for a while, not to sleep, she told herself, but only for a short rest, though she was worried that she might never get started again once she stopped.

At last she sat herself against a tall tree only a few yards from the path, pulling her blanket up over her head and tucking it closely around her. The tree was one of the papery ones that reminded her of birch trees except that its bark was the colour of bronze, looking almost red in the light that Saffi cast around them as he landed on the trunk and hung there above her head. A heavy frost had already formed on the grass, so Lindy sat on her now empty pack to protect herself from the wet and the cold. She tucked her legs up under the blanket against her chest and laid her head on her knees. The blanket now covered her completely, and the trees cut the wind quite well, and she began to feel warmer, though the pack beneath her was already a bit damp.

She had promised herself that she would not sleep, but she was more exhausted than she thought. Though she could not sleep exactly, because she would always begin falling to one side or another and then wake with a start, she certainly fell into the edges of sleep, drifting in half-dreams that seemed more real and more vivid than any dream. Hours may well have passed while she sat there, though she could not have said how many, and all the while she saw the most startling things.

Her mother and Alisdair appeared, their arms tied and their mouths gagged, but somehow they came to her anyway and hugged her and told her how much they missed her and sat down under the tree to talk with her. Lindy's mother was looking all around and saying how

159

beautiful everything was, just as if she was free and was sitting on the grass on a summer day to see the whole forest spread out before her, and Alisdair was saying that this had always been one of his favourite stretches of the road to the bridge, and that he was glad to have some friends along to share it with him. They both seemed perfectly content to sit among the trees and look at the scenery, never giving even the slightest notice to the ropes that bound their arms and legs or to the gags that filled their mouths. It was so very strange to hear the two of them talking like old friends and all the while to see them tied so strongly.

Lindy tried to go and free them, but her body was frozen in place, and she could only watch them, feeling more and more helpless and guilty. "I'm sorry," she cried, "I can't move. I'm trying to help you, but I can't move." Her mother was just remarking to Alisdair about how fresh the air was, and the two of them looked at Lindy in surprise.

"Oh, my Little Lady," Missus Merton said, which was something that she used to say when Lindy was very small and now said only when she thought Lindy was in particular need of comforting. "You don't have anything to be sorry for," she cried, but the sound of her voice coming from behind the gag in her mouth only upset Lindy still more. She struggled desperately to break whatever it was that was holding her, but she could not move even so much as her finger, and she could only watch as Alisdair and her mother gradually disappeared.

Then it seemed that she was drifting up above herself, only a little, just beneath the treetops, and the sun was shining brightly. She was flying between the trees, chasing something that was always just beyond her. She sometimes caught a glimpse of a brightness now and again, and she thought she must be following the sun or some other star, but then she knew that this light was much greater than any star and that it would blind her if she should ever catch sight of it. She tried to stop herself from following, but she kept hurtling faster and faster after the light, and then she could see a dense grove of trees far ahead that was shining with the brightness of a white hot fire. She closed her eyes, but the light passed through her eyelids, and the world seemed full only of brightness, but all at once everything was dark, and she was herself again, half-asleep beneath the tree.

Her first thought was that she should get up and begin her journey once more, but she was so tired, and soon she was drifting in her half-dream again. She found that she had become a great tree, looking out across a mighty forest as the rising sun made her red bark glint like bronze. She could feel how far and how deep her roots went beneath the forest floor, and she knew the secret names of every creature that lived among her branches and beneath her bark and between her roots. Then she saw that far away, at the edges of the great forest, there were great plumes of smoke, and there were deep tremors in

161

the earth, and she saw a thousand creatures cutting the trees with impossible speed, burning them and leaving them to rot, and she felt fear in the forest itself. Soon the axes were at her own trunk, but the blows would not harm her, and for a moment she felt relief, until she looked around her to see only an unending wasteland from horizon to horizon where not even a single other tree survived, and she knew that she was now alone.

She was filled with a great sadness, as though her whole world was dying piece by piece. Still more visions passed before her eyes, but she could remember nothing of them afterwards, only the feeling of loneliness that hung over everything. Each dream seemed to offer some hope, but it was always a hope that lay just beyond her reach or came at too great a cost, and each dream seemed to be a part of all the others, until they became one long vision of hopelessness. At last, she found herself hovering above the ground in a wide forest not far from an overgrown road, and she saw something lying beneath a tree, lit by a glow that seemed to come from the tree itself, and she knew that this was no dream, that it was her own self huddled beneath the blanket on the cold ground below, and she knew also that she needed to wake herself and continue on her journey. She tried to shake the huddled figure below her, but her hands passed right through her own body. She cried out, but her voice was as feeble as her touch, and the weight of her visions hung over her, and she began to wonder whether things would

162

end as badly as her dreams seemed to foretell.

Just then there was the sudden sound of wings, and birds were settling all around her, turning into women as they landed. Lindy could see Cleanna among them, and then she was herself again, and she felt hands gently shaking her to wakefulness beneath her blanket. She let herself be bundled and carried along by arms much stronger than her own, and in what seemed like only a few minutes more the hooves of horses could be heard clattering on the road, and a small open carriage drew up with Clinton holding the reins and looking as grave and concerned as his propriety allowed him. Lindy felt herself being lifted into the carriage, and then Cleanna was beside her, wrapping a heavy blanket around them both. Lindy laid her head on the bird-woman's shoulder, feeling warmer and safer already.

In Which Clinton Holds a Council

When Lindy woke the next morning, the first thing she saw was the thatch of a cottage ceiling, and she thought for a moment that she was back in Amena's cottage. It was only when she sat up and saw Clinton sitting in a chair beside the bed, his face full of concern, that she remembered what had happened the night before and began to wonder exactly where she was.

"Oh," said Clinton, as soon as he saw she was awake, and he resumed his impassive expression, straightening himself in his chair. "You're awake," he said, and he looked at her uncomfortably, as if trying to guess how much she had seen.

Lindy sat back against the wall and tucked her legs up against her chest. "On behalf of everyone at The Crofts," Clinton said, trying to recover his usual formality, "I would like to express our great relief that you are safely home at last." He looked away then, and he lowered his voice, letting ceremony drop again. "We feared the worst," he said. "Penates told us you were alive, but we thought you'd fallen into Khurshid's hands. And then all that rabble arrived at the bridge the day before last, and with Midsummer so soon, we were losing hope."

"Amena saved me," said Lindy, but she realized that Clinton would not likely know who Amena was, so she added, "I mean, the woman in the cottage saved me." There was a buzzing of wings from the foot of her bed, and Lindy noticed that Saffi was sitting by her feet. "Well," she tried again, "I guess it was Saffi here who actually saved me." The insect folded his wings and nestled into the blankets again. "He took me to the cottage that I saw in my vision," she continued, "and there was a woman there called Amena. She was the one who helped me."

Clinton stood. "Yes, I'd like to hear the whole of your story," he said, "but I should first call the others so they can hear it as well. I can have Penates send some food too, if you like. Would you eat something if I brought it, Miss Lindy."

"Oh, yes," said Lindy, who felt, what was true, that she had eaten only winter apples and bread and a few wild strawberries for two days running.

Clinton left through the cottage's low, wooden door, leaving Lindy alone with Saffi. The insect half-flew from the bottom of the bed to land on Lindy's lap, nuzzling itself against her and making low clicking sounds, and Lindy realized at once that it was saying goodbye.

"Good bye to you too," she whispered. She was surprised at how melancholy she was to be losing the little creature, like at the end of summer camp when she had to say goodbye to her friends for another year, but she knew that Amena needed a companion too, and she did not begrudge him going. Saffi lifted into the air and dipped low in what might have been a bow. Then he nudged his way through the window and was gone, leaving Lindy feeling very much more alone than before.

She took a deep breath and tried to distract herself by having a look around her. She had already guessed that she was not in The Crofts, neither in her bedroom nor in her cubby, but in a cottage very much like Amena's, and now she began to wonder if she had been sleeping in one of the empty cottages that she had first seen when she came to The Weald. She had looked through the windows then, and she thought she remembered the small stone fireplace and the plain wooden furniture, and the little loft right above her bed. The whole room had the same familiar feeling, as if she had been there before.

She had only just finished taking stock of these surroundings when the cottage door opened again, and there entered a whole flock of visitors, first Cleanna, and then a few faces that Lindy recognized from her time in The Crofts but could not actually name, and then more faces that she could not remember ever having seen before.

The cottage was not really big enough to hold everyone, so some had to give way in order for others to have their turn, and for several minutes it seemed that someone was always coming and someone was always going and someone was always saying how good it was to see her safely back. Though Lindy was worried at first that they would be angry, everyone was very kind, and nobody said anything at all about Moe or Khurshid or the crown.

When at last everyone had been able to see Lindy and give their best wishes, the cottage began to empty, leaving only Clinton and Cleanna and a few others behind. There was the blind woman who had sat with Lindy at the breakfast table on the morning Alisdair had been captured; and there was a broad, muscled woman with thick, dark hair; and there was also a beautiful young man, very short and slender and delicate, a perfectly formed man only a little taller than Lindy herself. They all sat talking quietly as Lindy finished the breakfast that Clinton had brought and that she had been too distracted to eat until now, waiting expectantly until she had eaten her last bite.

"Miss Lindy," said Clinton then, tugging at his cuffs and turning to the small group around the table, "You already know Cleanna, of course, but these others are perhaps new to you." He gestured to the blind woman, who was seated just to the left of where he stood. "This is Nydia, one of the oldest of us here at The Crofts." Nydia inclined her head, smiling pleasantly, and her smooth eyes, which had been blank until then, began to show the rapidly changing symbols that Lindy recalled from their first meeting.

"This," said Clinton, turning to the woman with the broad shoulders and muscled arms, "is Bayard. She came to join us for the great feast, but she feared the worst even then and decided to stay and lend her aid if anything should happen. She will lead those who choose to resist Khurshid by force of arms."

Clinton then turned to the last of the party, the diminutive man. "And this is Freidan," he continued. "He is one of those with whom Alisdair consulted about the arch. He has come to us with news about what may be happening to the arch and to The Crofts, all of which we will share with you in due time." He looked back to Lindy. "Penates would like to have joined us also, of course, but he is unable to leave his kitchens, and he tells us that The Crofts will not permit you to enter its doors, so we must make do without him for the moment, though we can consult him very easily should it be necessary. Now, though I don't want to impose too much on you, especially considering what you've endured over the last few days, it's already quite late in the morning, and much remains to be done to prepare for Midsummer tonight, so might we ask you to relate as much of your tale as you are able."

Lindy set aside her plate and swung her legs over the edge of the bed, trying to think of where to begin.

Her first thought was that she should tell the story right from the morning that she and Moe and Cleanna had set out from The Crofts, but she had only just begun when Clinton interrupted politely to say that Cleanna had already told them the story that far. Lindy asked exactly how much Cleanna had been able to tell them, and so Cleanna ended up retelling some of her own story, explaining how she had outflown the traitor-kings and the forest night-fliers and escaped to The Crofts.

When she finished, Lindy tried to remember everything she could and to put things in their proper places, much as she did later when she was retelling the story for me, but she kept forgetting things and having to go back to fill in the details that she had missed, so it took her longer to tell the story than you might expect, the rest of the morning and into the afternoon in fact. Everyone was glad to hear that Moe had still been alive when she saw him last and that Alisdair was still alive as well, at least according to Khurshid, and they were all sympathetic when they heard that Lindy's mother was being held captive also. When she got to the part about Amena's cottage, Nydia said that she remembered having met the same Amena long ago, before Khurshid's country had become as dangerous as it was now, and Clinton said that there were others like Amena and that Alisdair would surely know her since he often went to visit these people and bring them what he could. It was the last part of Lindy's story that caused the most excitement, however, when she told them how Khurshid was bringing his prisoners to the bridge for Midsummer night.

"We must rescue them!" Cleanna cried, and the same emotion was written clearly on everyone's faces. No one, however, seemed to know exactly how such a thing could be managed, and there was a long silence in the room.

At last Clinton cleared his throat. "Now," he said, quietly and firmly, as though he were trying to convince himself as much as the others, "You all know I want to see Alisdair and Missus Merton rescued as much as anyone, and Moe too if he's there to be rescued, but I don't see any way it can be done, and unless someone else has an idea, we simply have no more time to spend thinking on it. There's too much to do between now and midnight. We must tell Lindy our plans, and then we must be about them." He looked around the room, from one person to another, and no one said anything. There was not a happy face among them, but at last everyone nodded in agreement, though Cleanna looked as though she would cry. Lindy could barely restrain her own tears, but she could think of nothing that might be done, so she nodded too, and she kept her eyes on the stone floor so that no one would see that they were glistening.

"Now," Clinton said, "to the point. Miss Lindy, in something less than eight hours, at midnight, Khurshid will cross the bridge, and there will be no Keeper remaining to prevent him. He will almost certainly make straight for The Crofts, and we do not have the strength to defend it for long."

"Some of us are preparing to resist him," interjected Bayard, and for a moment she seemed to become a huge black mare, muscles tensed and nostrils flared.

"Yes," continued Clinton, "Bayard will lead the more warlike among us to harass Khurshid's followers and to draw them away from the house for as long as possible, but there are none among us who can face Khurshid himself or the traitor-kings directly, so we must assume that The Crofts will fall to him before too long." Though he said this with his usual unflappable demeanour, his voice was grim, and no one else made so much as a noise to break the heavy silence when he paused.

"Since we cannot defend The Weald," he said at last, "then we must evacuate it in as orderly a fashion possible. There are some who will stay and keep their homes from Khurshid if they can, but the bird women have already been gathering those who wish to leave by the arch, and Nydia will supervise their evacuation to whichever world they choose." He looked around again. "We must be quick about it. The traitor-kings may not wait for midnight to attack us here, and they must not be allowed to capture the arch."

"Can't we close the arch to them or something?" asked Lindy

"I'm not sure that it would do any good," replied Clinton, "but Freidan can explain much better than I." He looked at the diminutive man pointedly. "I will ask

171

him to keep it short."

"Certainly," said Freidan, his voice seeming larger than he was, a full and rich voice. "I've had some time to examine the arch closely," he said, "and I don't think that the traitor-kings came into The Crofts through the arch at all. I think what's happened is that The Weald has become tied too closely to Alisdair's world, to your world, Miss Lindy. The Weald takes its shape from the worlds of the Keepers who protect it, and Alisdair has been the only Keeper for so long that his world and this one have been drawing closer and closer together. I think that's why the traitor-kings were able to enter The Weald that day. They didn't cross the veil. They passed directly from this world into Alisdair's, where there is no veil. Once they were there, they entered Alisdair's property and passed back to this world, directly into The Crofts."

"They can do that?" Lindy exclaimed.

"They couldn't before," Freidan answered, "but I believe they can now, though Khurshid himself must not be able to travel like this, or he would be here even now. I think that he must have discovered how the two worlds were coming together and sent the traitor-kings to go into Alisdair's world to watch the arch and to capture him there where his power is weaker."

"So, are they still there?" interrupted Lindy again, "In my world, I mean?"

"We believe so," replied Freidan. "This is why we must evacuate everyone as quickly as possible, so that

172

they don't become trapped here when the traitor-kings pass into The Crofts from Alisdair's house."

"Cleanna's people," interjected Nydia, "have been gathering those who wish to leave for two days now, and some have left already. A few are choosing to stay, I know, but we will help any who want to leave until it looks as though the arch is in danger of being captured." She looked as if she would say more, but then hesitated.

"And then," finished Freidan, his rich voice heavy with determination, "then I will destroy the arch."

— 20 —

In Which Lindy Has Words with The Crofts

When everyone had finally gone to do the things that needed to be done, Lindy was left to dress and make herself as presentable as she could. She had only the same clothes that she had been wearing for days, the same ones that had been torn in the forest and mended by Amena and dirtied by a day and most of a night of walking. Even when she dusted them off, they still looked like she had found them in the trash, and she was almost glad that there was no mirror in the cottage to show how tangled her hair was. She ran her fingers through the knots to try and straighten them, but she doubted that it improved things much, and she was too worried about her mother and about everything else to really care about her hair anyway.

There was really not much else for her to do though, so she went to the door and laid her hand on the latch, but she was not sure whether she was ready to see anyone quite yet. It was as though she was feeling every emotion at once. She had been so relieved to be back at The Crofts and so happy to see everyone again and so certain that they would find a way to rescue her mother and Alisdair, but now it looked as though there would be no rescue after all, and all her happiness was mixed with anger and frustration and disappointment and despair. All she really wanted to do was to stay hidden away in the cottage until everything was over, but somehow she lifted the latch anyway, and somehow she found herself stepping out into the midday sunlight, and somehow she managed not to cry or scream or do any of the things that you and I would probably have done if we were her.

Outside the cottage, people of every shape and description had settled themselves around the arch and its platform. They looked like the pictures that Lindy had seen in newspapers of refugees from wars or disasters, huddling in small groups and clutching a few things too precious to leave behind. Their faces were all tired and worried and frightened, and Lindy began to realize just how many lives she had put at risk by losing the crown. She had never imagined that so many people lived in The Weald. There had been a good many at the feast in the great hall, of course, but they had mostly come from other worlds, and The Crofts had otherwise seemed so empty and lonely right from the moment that Lindy had first wandered among its cottages. Now it was over-flowing with people waiting their turn to go through the arch to places that Lindy could only guess at.

Even so, The Crofts still felt lonely to Lindy. Maybe it was because there was still no one to live in the cottages, or maybe it was because there would soon be no one left to live in The Weald at all, or maybe it was because Lindy herself was so terribly alone, but she felt the same sense of sadness about the cottages that she had felt when she first saw them, and she also felt the same sense that she belonged to them somehow, even if she could not protect them.

Clinton and Nydia were already waiting beside the arch. Lindy watched as a group of refugees approached them, and there was the now familiar shimmer in the arch, and the platform was empty once more. Clinton looked up and motioned for Lindy to join him, but everything felt wrong. She knew that it made perfect sense to send everyone away to safer places and to destroy the arch before Khurshid could use it, but she could not bring herself to believe that there was no other way. If only she could speak to Alisdair or Amena or Penates, or even The Crofts, anyone who might help her know what to do.

"Hello, Lindy," Clinton said, "would you help Nydia organize those who are leaving?"

"Yes, please," called Nydia, "I could really use your help."

There was nothing so very upsetting about what Clinton and Nydia had said, and Lindy knew that they probably intended only to make her feel useful and included, but for some reason it made her furious, and being furious over something so unreasonable made her even more furious, but it only took her a moment to realize that she was really only angry with herself for not having done what she knew she needed to do. She had been so caught up in everyone being kind and not blaming her for what had happened that she had forgotten why she had come back in the first place. Whatever anyone else said, and however much she wanted to believe them, Lindy knew that this whole situation was her own fault, and she knew also that she needed to face up to it, and that meant going to apologize to The Crofts, however hard it might be.

"No!" she said, more sharply than she intended. Nydia looked surprised at her tone. "I mean, I'm sorry," she said, "but there's something I need to do."

Lindy suddenly felt much better, and she realized just how much she had been dreading her meeting with The Crofts, and how much she had been trying to avoid it, and how guilty she had been feeling for not being brave enough to do it after she had come all this way.

She turned toward the house, along the same path where Clinton and Moe had led her when she had first arrived. The grass was much more trampled than it had been then, and there were now many voices to break the stillness that she had felt that morning, but there

177

was still something mysterious and unnerving about that walk, as though it would never end in the same place or in the same way twice. When she reached the door of the house, it seemed more than just an ordinary door to her. It seemed like a door that might lead anywhere, like the wardrobe in *The Lion, the Witch, and the Wardrobe* or like the mirror in *Lilith* or like the arms of the angel in *The Garden Behind the Moon.* "If I go through that door," she thought, "anything might happen," but then she remembered that going through the arch and climbing the long stairway and crossing the bridge had been much the same, and she felt a little better, so she reached for the handle.

As soon as she touched it, The Crofts filled every bit of her like an electric shock. She was frozen, unable either to open the door or to take her hand away.

"How dare you come back here?" the house roared through her mind. "You have destroyed me, and now you come to my door and ask my hospitality?" Lindy felt her body shaking with the house's rage. "You are a liar," it cried, "a liar and a traitor and a fool! And I was the greater fool for trusting you!"

Lindy tried desperately to focus her mind on calming The Crofts as she had done before, but the emotion of the house overwhelmed her. She could not even find the strength to speak, and her mind was overrun by emotions and images that were not her own. She knew that she was still there at the door, holding the handle in her hand, but she was also running among the cottages of The Crofts as huge and terrible creatures chased her through the burning buildings, smoke and ashes filling the air and screams ringing out everywhere around her. Then she was desperately holding back the door of The Crofts as it was rent from its hinges, throwing her back against the wall to watch Khurshid step across the threshold.

"You brought this on me!" the house screamed. "You gave the last crown to him, and now he's coming, and I'm ruined. Look! Look at what you've done."

All Lindy could see was fire and smoke and darkness and falling rubble. She was in the library with its books torn and scattered, fire licking at the doorframes, no way to escape but through the smoke-filled door. Then she was in the great hall, the long table smashed into kindling for a bonfire that rose almost to the vast ceiling, every horrible creature she could imagine dancing around it and throwing more fuel into its flames as she cowered in the corner trying to avoid their notice. A moment later she was in her own cubby, trapped against the window by a fire that was already consuming her few precious things and would force her either to jump from the window or suffocate in the smoke.

"Please," Lindy managed, "I'm sorry."

"Sorry?" raged the house. "Will sorry keep me from ruin?"

"It won't, I know. But I am sorry. Really. I did what I thought I should, but everything went wrong, and I'm

179

sorry. You were right. I just wasn't strong enough."

Suddenly the house's rage became sorrow, and the change shocked Lindy's mind all over again. She found herself crying with great sobs, and she would have fallen to the ground if her hand had not been fixed so firmly to the handle of the door. There flashed through her mind images of countless people, one after the other, and then she was among them. She recognized none of them, but she knew that they were Keepers and other residents of The Crofts from across the years. She walked with them among the cottages and feasted with them in the great hall and ate with them in the kitchens and watched plays with them in the theatre and read with them in the library and did all the other things with them that had made The Crofts a home. With each person she met, Lindy could feel the house's sadness, as if it was looking through photographs of old friends who had died, knowing that there would never be any more such friends, and she felt as though she might drown in the house's sorrow.

At last, Alisdair appeared among the rest. He was sitting solemn and kindly in a leather chair, and Lindy felt her own grief match the grief of The Crofts. "I'm sorry," she cried again, though she knew that Alisdair's loss had not really been her fault. "I didn't know."

"What do you want of me?" The Crofts demanded. "What can you possibly want of me now?"

"I want to keep my home from Khurshid, just like

Amena and Penates, and my cubby here is the only home I have now."

"This is not your home!" the house thundered, its renewed anger washing over Lindy's mind.

"I know," Lindy said, feeling just how true this was. "I know it's not really my home, but I thought at least the cubby could be my home. Couldn't it?"

All at once The Crofts became almost calm, and it spoke with a cold sternness. "A place is not your home just because it looks like your home, or just because you have put your things in it. You have to make a place your home. You have to do something to make it your home."

"What do I have to do?"

"Nobody can tell you what to do. You'll either know, or you won't. But this is not your home." The house paused for a moment, "and soon it will be nobody's home at all."

"Can't I at least go and get my things from my cubby?" Lindy asked. She felt tired all of a sudden, as if she had been standing there at the door for hours.

The Crofts hesitated a moment, then relented. "Take whatever you want. It makes no difference now."

At once, Lindy's hand was released from the door-knob, and she sank to her knees as her things appeared beside her. It looked like the whole contents of the attic were there, but most of them were not really important to her. All she wanted was her old sleeping bag and her favourite pillow that she used for propping herself up when she was reading. She had no idea what exactly she wanted with them. She told me later that even asking for her things had been a whim, and it was only after everything was sitting on the lawn that she felt how much she needed that blanket and that pillow, though she was still not sure why.

Still weak and trembling from her encounter with the house, she put herself back on her feet and walked over to her sleeping bag, rolled it up, and tucked it under one arm. Then she put her pillow under the other and set off down the path toward the bridge. She could not have told you exactly why she went in that direction, except that it seemed the only thing left to do.

— 21 —

In Which Things Get Much Worse Indeed

If you have ever noticed how the distance between one thing and another can change depending on how you are feeling, you will understand how Lindy felt as she walked to the bridge that afternoon. Her first walk from The Crofts to the bridge with Moe and Cleanna had gone by in a moment because her heart had been full of gladness and a glorious spring morning. This second time, however, with evening coming on, and with the weight of the house's despair, and with the fear of what Khurshid was about to do at midnight, the road seemed ever so much longer. The pillow and the blanket she was carrying were not very heavy, but they were bulky and awkward, so she was always stopping to readjust her grip or to switch arms. Though it was not nearly as cold as the night before, there was a cool breeze blowing, so she was a little cold too, and the road dragged on and on, so it was getting dark by the time Lindy came at last to the edge of the forest and looked out across the river valley.

She had been able to hear Khurshid's camp for some time already, and even from across the river she could see fires burning everywhere, and the whole valley smelled of smoke and mud and rot and even nastier things. She was still not sure what she intended to do, but her feet seemed to follow the path, whether she willed them to or not, and the path led them down the hill and across the meadow and, without any hesitation, right to the highest point of the bridge. There she unrolled her sleeping bag and crawled into it, her back against the wall of the bridge, the sleeping bag pulled up around her, and the pillow tucked between her head and the cold stone.

It was not yet quite dark, and it soon became clear that Lindy's presence on the bridge had not gone unnoticed. At first there were only a few shouts and pointing fingers in the midst of the general noise and chaos in the valley below, but soon there were more and more people looking up to where she was sitting. The meadow gradually quietened, and a crowd gathered at the foot of the bridge, and when there was nothing but silence across the valley, Khurshid himself stood on his carriage throne and looked up toward where Lindy lay.

"Welcome, Lindy," he called.

Lindy said nothing, just looked steadily into the clear evening sky, still grey with the last light of day.

"Are we no longer on speaking terms, dear Lindy?"

Khurshid mocked. "Very well, but we will speak later, and then you will answer me, I assure you."

Lindy still kept quiet. Khurshid's taunts no longer bothered her somehow, and the sky above her was too lovely to spoil with even a glance in his direction. The first stars were appearing, and her sleeping bag was growing nicely warm in the chill air. Though she was only a few short steps from her enemy, and though she was only a few short hours from watching him invade her adopted home, she was full of a strange peace. Maybe it was because she had finally faced up to The Crofts, or maybe it was because she knew that she had done all she could, or maybe it was because of something else entirely, but she knew somehow that she was where she should be, and she felt content despite everything. She still desperately wanted things to turn out right, of course, wanted her mother and Alisdair to be rescued more than anything, but her heart was at peace. It was not a feeling that she ever managed to describe to me, but anything worth feeling is like that, I think, so I did not ask her to explain any further, and you will have to content yourself with that as well.

Lindy was never sure if she actually slept there on the bridge that night, lying on the hard, smooth stone under the high, clear sky. She could not remember closing her eyes or falling asleep or waking up, but she did remember falling into something like a dream. She thought that she could see the constellations sail across the sky, and she felt like she was drifting too, just like the stars, as if the bridge had been picked up by a silent and tremendous wave and floated along among the cool, white lights of the night sky. The stars began to swirl, and there were ribbons of them gathered like mist, and Lindy felt only how small she was in the midst of everything. After a moment she realized that the stars looked familiar again, and it seemed to her that she was now in two places at once, both on the bridge in The Weald and also on the railway that ran down the middle of the street in front of her own house back home. She had the feeling that the two places were the same, that she was hovering between them, and that she could go home again that very minute if only she willed it. The idea tempted her, but only for a moment. She knew thst she could never abandon her mother and Alisdair, but it was comforting to feel that she was so close to home after all.

All at once, there was a shouting and a roaring and a beating of drums at the foot of the bridge, and Lindy found herself very much awake again. She scrambled out of her sleeping bag to her feet and looked down the curve of the bridge. Huge creatures had seized Khurshid's carriage by the bars along its sides and were dragging it step-by-step up the bridge, while the crowd pressed around it, waving torches and brandishing weapons and beating drums and playing horns. The procession moved slowly, but it was not long before it had come close enough for Lindy to see the faces of the beasts struggling to pull the vast carriage and to see Khurshid sitting sprawled on his throne.

She backed along the bridge a few steps, just to be sure that she had the veil between Khurshid and herself, and then she waited for him to come. She tried to think what she should do, but her mind was still distracted with everything she had just seen and with the feeling of being so close to her home, and she could not seem to make things come clear. If only the bridge was her home, she thought, then Khurshid wouldn't have any right to it, and this idea suddenly seemed to make perfect sense to her, though she had no idea how to go about making the bridge a home.

"Lindy!" she heard Khurshid cry, and there was a profound silence as the voices and the drums were stilled. He skipped lightly down to the very last stair of the carriage, his lithe body glinting in the torchlight, and he held out his hand to her. "Come up to my throne, my dear. I have something to show you."

"You can show me from there," Lindy called back, her voice much braver than she felt.

Khurshid threw back his head and laughed aloud. He motioned grandly in the air with his hand and began slowly to remount the stairs of the throne as a small group of figures made their way from the dim mass behind the carriage into the light of the throne's torches. Though Lindy already hoped that her mother and Alisdair and Moe would be among the group, she still cried

187

aloud when she finally made out their faces as they were shoved roughly to the stairs of the carriage. The lights and the crowd and even Khurshid himself all but disappeared from Lindy's mind, and in their place was only her mother and Alisdair and Moe. She could not even remember afterwards what it was that she shouted when she first saw them, only that she ran across the veil, no longer caring whether she was putting herself into danger, and she threw her arms around her mother.

If anyone said anything for the next few minutes, Lindy never knew, and if they did anything, she never knew that either. All she knew was the warmth of her mother's face and the smell of her hair and the sound of her voice murmuring from behind the gag. It was as if time stopped for a moment, and Lindy found herself wishing that it would stop forever, even as the rest of the world began to return to her and as she began to remember once again exactly how serious a predicament they were still in.

It was only then that she heard Khurshid speak again, much closer and much softer. "I'm so glad you like your surprise, Lindy. I knew you would." He looked mockingly down at her.

A gong sounded then, a huge, deep sound that seemed to come from the earth itself, and everyone looked up startled to see a vast sheet of dancing colour, like the northern lights that Lindy sometimes saw at her grandfather's cottage up north. The colours were in long streaks that reached up from the centre of the river all along its length, splitting the bridge at its highest point and reaching as far as the eye could see into the night sky.

"The veil!" Khurshid cried, and his eyes looked wildly joyful. He turned back to Lindy. "It will soon be time," he said, "and I think we've had quite enough of this scene for now, don't you darling? It's time that you took your seat to watch my triumph."

Lindy saw two figures approaching from the sides of the carriage, the feline woman she had seen the night before and a tall, thin man who walked on all fours like a lizard, balancing on his tail when he stood. She did not know how much time was left until midnight, but she knew that it must now be short, and so she knew that her own time was short as well. She tried desperately to think what could be done, but her mind was filled only with Amena's voice. It seemed to be saying, "Make the bridge your home," again and again, only she had no idea how.

She felt the lizard-man put his hand on her shoulder, and she flinched back instinctively. "Get away!" she cried, because there was nothing else she could do. "This bridge is my home! You can't touch us here!"

The lizard-man shrunk back for a moment, and the woman paused as well, shifting into the shape of a spotted, black panther, but Khurshid only laughed. "You foolish girl," he snarled. "A place isn't your home because you throw a few blankets on the ground and say so." He stalked down the stairs, seized her arm, and jerked her to her feet. "Now," he said, "you will sit where you're told, and you would be wise not to interrupt me again tonight."

He dragged her up the stairs of the carriage and threw her down at the foot of his throne against the chest of crowns, then seated himself on his throne. The crowd still waited silently, and Lindy kept quiet too, looking down past the heap of crowns in the open chest to where her mother and Alisdair and Moe were tied at the foot of the carriage. She knew that this was the end of things for them and for her and for The Crofts, but she could not really bring herself to believe it. Everything had turned out wrong, despite her best intentions. She had followed her visions and only lost the crown. She had gone back to face The Crofts and only been rejected. She had tried to make the bridge her home and only been captured. She had failed time after time, and now there would be no more chances to make it right.

"If only," she said, so quietly that even she could hardly hear herself, "if only Alisdair had never given me the crown." She said this only absently, without meaning much by it, but she happened to say it just as her eyes were on Alisdair's crown where it sat atop all the others in the chest below her, and she found herself wondering what might happen if she were to put the crown back on Alisdair's head right that moment. She turned her head very slightly to the left, just enough to see that the tall, reptilian man was still standing guard over her, and she could only assume that the panther-woman was standing behind her as well. She had no time to think any further, however, because just then there was a rippling shout that began at the furthest flanks of the great crowd and swelled to its centre, almost like the wave at a baseball game.

Lindy could not at first understand what had caused the outcry, but she soon saw that the veil of light was being eaten up at both ends by a ripple of silver flame, like a sparkler burning from both ends, moving ever closer to the bridge from each side. The flame moved slowly, but Lindy guessed that it would only be minutes before the two waves of silver met at the bridge and the veil of lights was eaten up entirely.

"At last!" she heard Khurshid shout to the crowd behind her. "The veil falls, and there is no one to renew it!" Another roar went up, and Lindy turned to see that Khurshid was now standing on his throne and looking back across the screaming throng below him. The moment seemed never to end, Khurshid standing with his head thrown back and his arms outspread, the horde below him roaring its lunatic pleasure, and Lindy feeling as though all hope had at last been exhausted. It was in that same moment, however, when everything seemed to wait, when the noise was deafening, and when everyone's attention was fixed on Khurshid, that a very different kind of shouting rose up from the direction of the veil.

191

Though Lindy was sitting right in the midst of everything, she was never very clear about what happened, and I had to ask some of the others in order to learn exactly what took place that night. It seems that Bayard had led The Croft's more warlike creatures to surprise Khurshid when he crossed the bridge, creeping down across the meadow under the cover of darkness and hiding in the long grass at the foot of the bridge. Then, as they were waiting, Khurshid had stood on his throne to address his army, and Bayard had seized the momentary distraction to rush upon his followers.

This is why, when Lindy turned to the commotion behind her, she saw the whole width of the bridge filled with the creatures of The Crofts falling on Khurshid's vanguard with sword and tooth, shield and claw. Bayard stood in the middle of them, a massive black mare with shaggy fetlocks and hooves shod with sharp, killing shoes. She reared up above the fray, striking out with her forelegs, her enemies falling before her, and Lindy thought for a moment that perhaps the day might be saved, that Alisdair might be rescued, and that everything might be set right, but it was only for a moment.

From around the carriage on both sides there streamed Khurshid's host. Where they had felt wrong to Lindy in the daylight, they felt hideous to her now, with their howling mouths and their malevolent eyes and their glinting weapons. They threw themselves wildly at Bayard and her companions, striking each other as much as their enemies and seeming not to care how many of their own were struck down. They drove forward by the sheer weight of their numbers, and soon the traitor-kings were among them as well, too powerful to be resisted, and before long even Bayard was forced to give ground.

Lindy saw now that the attack must fail, that the prisoners would not be saved, and at first her heart succumbed to hopelessness, but her eyes fell again on the chest of crowns, and she seized on one last hope. The traitor-kings who had been standing guard over her had rushed down to the bottom of the carriage to protect it from anyone who chanced to come that far, and Khurshid himself was still standing on his throne, looking intently at the struggle that would soon force Bayard and the others back past the veil. There was no one, in other words, paying any attention to Lindy, and she knew that she must either act now or not at all. Though she had no idea if it would actually help anything, and though she was almost certain that she would be caught and punished before she could even manage it, she darted forward, seized Alisdair's crown from the golden casket, and ran down the steps of the carriage. Then she set the crown on its rightful owner's head.

— 22 —

In Which There Are Two Remarkable Happenings

When Lindy placed the crown on Alisdair's head, two quite different but equally remarkable things began happening at exactly the same time.

One of those things happened right before Lindy's eyes, and it was the thing that everyone else saw as well, once they realized that something was going on and turned to find what it was. All at once Alisdair's chains dropped away, and he came to his feet without ever seeming to stand, and he became the king that Lindy had first seen coming through the arch in Mister Hat's garden, stern and beautiful and terrible. His green-gold face seemed almost to glow, and the patterns on his robes danced and swirled around him. He had no sword, only a golden branch, topped with leaves of many colours, orange and yellow, green and silver, red and gold, but he held it before him like a weapon.

In only a moment, he had reached the top of the stairs, though he hardly seemed to move. Khurshid's guards recognized the danger too late, and though the feline woman sprang at him with clawed hands, and though the lizard-man drew a long sinuous blade, Alisdair only motioned with the branch, and they fell aside as if they had been struck by some huge and invisible fist. Khurshid, however, made no attempt to attack, standing tall and still on his throne, and Lindy felt as though the world was balanced between them, waiting on what would happen next.

"You will leave now," Alisdair told him. There was neither anger nor fear in his voice, only a steady calm, and as he spoke, he casually bent to close the chest of crowns, as if he were merely tidying up around the house while speaking to an unruly child.

Khurshid gave no answer, but seemed to gather himself, his eyes glittering like gems and his hair lit red-gold in the torchlight, and then he flung himself into the air, high over Alisdair's head, caught himself on broad wings, and fell upon Lindy in an instant, seizing her in one arm and holding a knife to her throat with the other. Then he turned to face Alisdair again.

Now, as I said, this was one of the things that began happening when Lindy returned the crown to Alisdair, but there was a second thing, a very different thing, but just as important in its way. You see, in the same instant that Lindy put the crown on Alisdair's head, the same instant that he was freed from his chains, Lindy made quite an astonishing realization. Somehow, without quite knowing what she was doing, she had done what needed to be done, and everything changed for her. She saw quite clearly, for the first time, what it meant really to do something. It was not that she was the only one who could have given the crown back to Alisdair, or that she had been somehow destined to do it, or even that she had needed to do it. She had just been in a time and place where something needed to be done, and she had done it. More importantly, she also knew, not in her mind only but also in her spirit, that this thing she had done had made the place her home at last, had made all The Weald her home in a way, but the bridge in particular, made it her home in a sense that she could not hope to describe. She had laid her things in the middle of the bridge, and she had claimed it, and now she had done something to make it what she claimed.

This is why, when Khurshid swooped down and seized her, Lindy was not at all afraid. Though she was still not quite clear about what had happened, she was already certain that there was no longer anything to fear, and even as she saw Alisdair hesitate where he stood between Khurshid's throne and the golden chest, she did not hesitate herself, only spoke out with a clear, strong voice. "Let me go," she said, as firmly and boldly as she had ever said anything, and she felt Khurshid flinch.

"I'll do no such..." he started to say, but Lindy could already feel his grip loosening despite himself, and he gave a roar of surprise and anger. "What magic is this?" he screamed, his hands now pulling completely free of his prey.

Lindy turned to look into his eyes. "This is my home," she said, for the second time that night, "and you must leave."

He held her gaze for a few seconds longer, and Lindy could feel him struggling against the truth of what she had said, and then he howled in rage, the howl of a beast. He sprang backward, taking the shape of a lion, and dashed up the steps of the carriage. Lindy thought for a moment that he would strike at Alisdair, but he only rushed past him and off the carriage in a single leap, and by the time Lindy reached the top of the steps, he was already fleeing between his followers down the road toward the forest.

A great silence fell over the river valley then. Even the breeze died away, and the torches burned tall and bright.

"Hear me now!" Alisdair called into the stillness, his voice filling the valley, seeming to come from everywhere, like a distant thunder. "I am a Keeper of The Weald, and I have met your master at the bridge as it was appointed that I should, and your master has fled." His voice had taken on a formal tone, as if he was reciting something

197

at a ceremony. He paused, and there was a murmur now, as those gathered in the valley below began to wonder at what had happened on the bridge above them. "What is more," Alisdair continued, "he has left behind him the crowns of the Keepers, so those of you who once wore them, those who betrayed them into his hands, are no longer bound to him. You need no longer be his servants, though it lies with you now to choose another way."

The murmuring of the crowd had become almost a roar, but Alisdair paid it no attention. "See," He demanded, "Midsummer is come, and the veil has been renewed."

Lindy saw a bright light shine out from behind her, and she looked to see that the two waves of silver fire had come together to make a great ball of flame in the centre of the bridge. The flame flickered and rose and grew brighter, towering into the sky, and then there was nothing. There was only a darkness, a darkness so deep that the torches from the valley below could do nothing to dispel it. How long the darkness remained, Lindy could not afterwards say, but it was suddenly split by a ball of silver fire once more, and then a wave of silver rushed out in both directions, leaving a veil of dancing colours behind it, like the joined tails of twin comets.

Behind her, Lindy heard the crowd crying out and rushing away in confusion, but she never looked back, only ran down the steps into her mother's arms.

— 23 —

In Which Some Final Things are Settled

The walk home from the bridge seemed like a dream to Lindy, because she could not quite bring herself to believe that it was true. Bayard had sent the fastest in her army to take news to The Crofts, while those who remained went on at a more leisurely pace, carrying the wounded and the fallen with them. Lindy and her mother and Alisdair and Moe went quietly at first, each with their own thoughts, but then they began to tell each other their stories, and soon they were laughing and crying and carrying on like the oldest of friends. Their spirits raised as they walked and as they began to realize just how great a victory had been won that night, and the whole procession soon took up their mood, so that before long they were shouting and singing and generally making the biggest party that Lindy had ever seen.

They arrived at The Crofts while it was still quite

early in the morning. The sun had not yet even brushed the horizon, and the cool of night still clung to everything, but they found everyone very much awake. The doors of the house all stood open, and the windows all shone with light. The cottages were all alight as well, and there was a great bonfire burning in the common between them. People were coming and going between the house and the fire, and they were all carrying food and drink to set at tables that had been dragged from the cottages. Others were playing music or singing and dancing, as if they were celebrating every holiday rolled into one.

Lindy was too tired really to join in the merriment, but she found a spot with her mother at one of the tables, and she ate a little of the feast being laid out for them, and she laid her head down on her hands to let the revelry swirl around her. She closed her eyes and felt her mother's hand on her shoulder and smelled the fire burning and heard some kind of pipe playing a song like a bubbling river, and she fell asleep in the midst of it all.

When she awoke it was just morning, the sun rising on a day that was still cool but that promised to grow hot. Everything was very quiet, and Lindy could see people sleeping all around her, sitting at the tables or lying on the grass or resting against the cottages. In fact, there was no one awake, as if everyone had fallen asleep all at once in the midst of their celebration, like the castle in *Sleeping Beauty*. Even her mother was asleep at the table beside her.

Lindy did not try to wake the sleepers, but she felt wide awake herself, so she got to her feet and began slowly walking the path to the house, the long grass now pressed flat by the passing of countless feet. She had set out in the direction of the house idly, because it was where the path naturally led, so she was halfway there before she remembered that she was no longer welcome at The Crofts. When she looked up at the house, however, the side door stood open, and she could imagine the little coat room through it and the kitchen beyond that, and she felt a longing to be back there again. Surely The Crofts would not forbid her now, she thought, not after everything had come out right at the bridge. Besides, if she could be brave enough to face Khurshid, she could certainly be brave enough to face the house, so she gathered herself and walked to the door and called out softly with her mind.

"Crofts," she asked, "May I come in?" The house did not answer, but she could feel it at the edges of her mind, full of emotion, happiness and embarrassment, gratitude and uncertainty, joy and fear. "I know how you feel," Lindy ventured again. "I'm not really sure what to say either, but it would make me very happy if we could just start over again."

There was a long moment when Lindy wondered whether the house would ever answer her, and then it said, "Come in," very quickly, as if a little ashamed, but Lindy felt a swell of happiness in The Crofts, and she knew that things would be better now.

She stepped across the threshold into the coat room with a heart lighter than any time she could remember, reaching out to brush her hands along the walls as she passed them, thinking back to when she had first come this way, when Clinton and Moe had frightened her half to death by changing into strange creatures before her eyes. She nudged open the door of the kitchen, expecting to see Penates already at work, but even he was asleep at his hearth, and the room stood empty except for two people sitting at the long, rough kitchen table. One of them was Alisdair, sitting back in his chair, his legs crossed and his hands holding a cup of tea in his lap, as if he was in the middle of a chat with an old friend. The other was a man whom Lindy had never seen before. At least, he was a man when she first saw him, young and handsome with light hair, but almost immediately he became a much older man, white-haired and bent with age, and then a moment later he became a young girl, not much older than Lindy herself, and the moment after that she became a middle-aged man with deep red skin and golden eyes. The figure took on one shape after another, each only for a second or two, so that Lindy thought that it must eventually look like every person who had ever lived, and she wondered whether it had ever looked like her, even just once.

"Welcome, Lindy," said Alisdair. He stood, and so

did the other person, who looked now like a poor woman dressed all in rags. "This is Aigonz. He is the spirit of this world, as The Crofts is the spirit of this house, and as you are the spirit of your body. He is The Weald itself, you might say." He bowed his head in Aigonz' direction as he said this, and Lindy bowed her head too, not only because Alisdair had done so, but because she felt somehow that Aigonz was someone to whom bows were rightfully due.

Aigonz came toward her, taking the form of a dark-skinned man with a broad smile and a carefully pressed suit. He put his hand out to Lindy. "I'm very glad to meet you, Lindy," he said. "You've done a great good here, and I am truly thankful to you."

"I only did what seemed like the right thing," Lindy said, feeling a little embarrassed.

"That is the only thing worth doing," Aigonz answered, becoming a small boy in a white robe, "and many are unable to do so much. Each of us, you and Alisdair and I, and even Khurshid, only ever need do what seems right, and no one may do it for us. We either do it, or we do not." He looked Lindy in the eyes. "This is not only the task of gods and heroes. It is the task that faces us all. We have no other."

"But I don't always know what the right thing is," said Lindy quietly.

"None of us ever do," replied Aigonz, now a beautiful young woman with chocolate skin and long black hair.

Her voice was gentle. "You can only keep watching and listening, and you will know it when it comes."

"I see," said Lindy, but she felt a bit overwhelmed.

Aigonz smiled, her white teeth flashing. Come," she said "let me show you what you've helped accomplish." Her hand was still outstretched, and Lindy came toward her and took it. There was a sound like a sudden gust of wind, and then the kitchen disappeared, and all three of them were standing in the great room at the top of the house. The places at the royal table had all been set with gold and with crystal, and there were tall candles, and boughs of fir, and wreaths of ivy. On every plate there was a crown, and they seemed alive to Lindy, as if they were filled with a joy of their own.

Aigonz had become a pale man with a scar that blinded him in one eye. "Do you see the crowns, Lindy" he asked. "They are all in their places once again, and soon Keepers will come from all the worlds, one by one, and they will take up the crowns, and The Crofts will be filled with people once again." As he said this, Lindy's mind was filled with images of the house bursting with people, coming and going and living together. She saw people laughing around the kitchen tables and hanging laundry outside the cottages and hoeing rows of vegetables in the fields, and there, in the midst of them, she also saw her mother, chopping vegetables in the kitchen, and she saw herself, standing on the bridge, looking out across the river valley.

Lindy was so filled with happiness that she could hardly speak, but she somehow kept from crying and looked up into Aigonz' eyes. "So," she managed, "does this mean that I can stay? And my Mom too?"

Aigonz nodded, his eyes becoming those of a shy-looking girl in floral-print dress. "Of course," she said.

"Will we live in my cubby?" Lindy asked.

The little girl laughed, and it sounded like a thousand laughs joined gently together, babies gurgling and children giggling and grandparents chuckling all at once. "Not exactly," she said. "Come, and I will show you." She took Lindy's hand again, and there was the same sound of wind, and they appeared now at the centre of the bridge. The morning sun glistened on the waters, and the trees moved gently, full of their summer leaves, and the sky was a light, morning blue. It was so beautiful that Lindy could hardly believe it was the same place where such terrible things had happened the night before.

"You won't be staying in your cubby," Aigonz said from beside her, "because this bridge, if you'll remember, is now your home." She had become now a very handsome young man, and Lindy quickly let go of his hand, feeling a little embarrassed.

"But we can't live here, can we?" she asked.

The handsome boy laughed his thousand laughs. "Can't you?" he said, but his voice was teasing. "Though you didn't know it, Lindy, you've become something that has never been seen in The Weald before. There have

205

been Keepers ever since Khurshid betrayed his home, and they were set to meet Khurshid at the bridge each year, so the veil could be renewed. But you have made the bridge your home, like a second seal on Khurshid's prison. So I'm making you a house here where you have already made your home, and you will keep watch over the bridge." He laughed again. "Yes, we've long had Keepers, but now we have a Watcher as well, and the Watcher needs a house."

He motioned with his hands, and the whole valley trembled. Stones rose from the ground, shaking free from the earth. Trees toppled along both banks. Everywhere there was the sound of rocks cracking and wood splitting, as the very stuff of the valley transformed itself into masonry and timber. All of it came flowing up the bridge in a rush, like water running uphill, and it joined itself together, stone on stone, timber on timber, until there stood before them a most beautiful house. Its foundations rested on the walls of the bridge, leaving a passage beneath it for people to pass, and it had a stairway leading up to a door in its floor, just like the one that led into Lindy's attic cubby.

"This will be your home," Aigonz said, looking now like a grey-haired woman with kind eyes. "Through its windows you can keep watch over the bridge, and through its door you may go to your cubby in The Crofts or in your own world any time you will it."

Lindy walked slowly toward the house, and set her

hand on the stair rail. A sense of rightness swept over her, and with it came visions that she knew would soon be true. She saw herself sitting at the kitchen table in The Crofts, sipping tea and talking with her friends. She saw her mother helping Penates at his labour, kneading bread and stirring soup and chopping vegetables. She saw the great hall prepared for a feast, a crowned Keeper at each place around the royal table. She saw herself in the library too, a book filling with words from an invisible hand as she told her story.

Then the visions passed. She climbed the stairs, pushed open the door, and knew at last that she was home.

About the Author

Jeremy Luke Hill is a husband and a father. He teaches literature, makes jams and preserves, reads continental philosophy, uses open source software, watches documentary film, grows trees from seed, and writes poetry, among other things. He keeps a blog at http://vocamus.net/jlh, and he can be reached at jeremylukehill@gmail.com.

www.ingramcontent.com/pod-product-compliance
Lightning Source LLC
Chambersburg PA
CBHW030324020726
47493CB00004B/1151